## "Why Are You Here?"

Michael's incredible blue eyes rolled heavenward, and Alexandra got the oddest feeling that he was expressing his feelings on a very personal level.

"Apparently," he muttered, "I've been had."

"What?"

"Somebody up there knows me too damned well."

He glared upward again, and Alex thought he looked oddly like a little boy tempting fate.

"Waiting for lightning to strike for one little curse word?" she asked mildly.

He looked back at her, startled. Then he laughed. "Something like that. You need some help around here."

"That," Alex said ruefully, "wouldn't take a genius to see. What does that have to do with you?"

He gazed at her steadily. "I'm here to help."

Dear Reader,

Happy holidays! At this busy time of year, I think it's extra important for you to take some time out for yourself. And what better way to get away from all the hustle and bustle of the season than to curl up somewhere with a Silhouette Desire novel? In addition, these books can make great gifts. Celebrate this season by giving the gift of love!

To get yourself in the holiday spirit, you should start with Lass Small's delightful *Man of the Month* book, *'Twas the Night*. Our hero has a plain name—Bob Brown—but as you fans of Lass Small all know, this will be no plain story. It's whimsical fun that only Lass can create.

The rest of December's lineup is equally wonderful. First, popular author Mary Lynn Baxter brings us a sexy, emotional love story, *Marriage, Diamond Style*. This is a book you'll want to keep. Next, Justine Davis makes her Silhouette Desire debut with *Angel for Hire*. The hero of this very special story is a *real* angel. The month is completed with stellar books by Jackie Merritt, Donna Carlisle and Peggy Moreland—winners all!

So go wild with Desire, and have a *wonderful* holiday season.

All the best,

Lucia Macro
Senior Editor

# JUSTINE DAVIS

## ANGEL FOR HIRE

SILHOUETTE *Desire*®

Published by Silhouette Books New York

**America's Publisher of Contemporary Romance**

SILHOUETTE BOOKS
300 East 42nd St., New York, N.Y. 10017

ANGEL FOR HIRE

ISBN: 0-373-05680-X

First Silhouette Books printing December 1991

Printed in the U.S.A.

**Books by Justine Davis**

Silhouette Desire

*Angel for Hire* #680

Silhouette Intimate Moments

*Hunter's Way* #371
*Loose Ends* #391
*Stevie's Chase* #402

---

## JUSTINE DAVIS

lives in San Clemente, California. Her interests outside of writing are sailing, doing needlework, riding and driving her restored 1967 Corvette roadster—top down, of course.

A policewoman, Justine says that years ago, a young man she worked with encouraged her to try for a promotion to a position that was, at that time, occupied only by men. "I succeeded, became wrapped up in my new job, and that man moved away, never, I thought, to be heard from again. Ten years later he appeared out of the woods of Washington state, saying he'd never forgotten me and would I please marry him? With that history, how could I write anything but romance?"

To my own Michael,
who is truly one of the very best people I know—
Your Alex is out there, somewhere;
don't ever settle for less than you deserve.

# Prologue

---

*"If this be magic, let it be an art*
*Lawful as eating."*

—Shakespeare
*The Winter's Tale*

"Please, help me to not give up."

The clouds swirled as the words drifted along on the wind, arriving with all of their poignancy intact. Words like these were not at all strange to this place, yet these got immediate attention.

"Now, that's a voice we've not often heard."

"True. She so rarely asks for anything."

"The last time, I believe, was with her brother."

"That was the only time, as I recall."

There was a rustling, then the same voice again. "Yes, that was it. Despite all her hardships, only the once."

"Yet she has an exemplary history. She could have asked for anything, and it would have been considered."

"And what she is trying to do is more of the same."

"So we're agreed? We send her the help she needs?"

"Absolutely."

There were nods all around.

"Who?"

"Ah, now there's a problem. We're spread a little thin at the moment."

"Gabriel?"

"No, he's still working on the Alden family. We've got to get that boy to speed things up."

"Yes. Make a note, will you? I'll look into it. Perhaps he needs some extra help. Now, what about Evangeline?"

"Still with that little girl. The child is having a terrible time. And everyone else is equally involved."

A collective sigh rose from the group. No words came for a moment, but all knew they had reached the same inevitable conclusion.

"We promised him a rest."

"I know. But what other choice do we have?"

"He is very tired."

"But she is very special."

"Oh, dear. He was so looking forward to a rest. He more than earned it after that thing with the two brothers."

"I don't blame him. They were horrible. If it hadn't been for their mother, I would have said let them kill each other and be done with it."

"It's just this one more time."

"That's what we told him last time."

"And the time before that."

"And before. But this time he swore he'd hold us to it."

"He wants a rest. A long one. And he deserves it. We've been draining his energy for a long time."

"We could help, give him a little more, a loan, so to speak."

"Too risky. We could burn him out altogether."

"Yes, and what would we do without him?"

"It's all academic. He won't go."

"Quiet, please." The new voice was stern, and hushed the chatter instantly. "You all seem to have forgotten something."

"What, sir?"

"Michael."

"Sir?"

"Perhaps I should say Michael's nature. His heart, the very thing that makes him the best we have."

"But even the greatest of hearts can be strained."

"Yes. But even Michael himself doesn't know his own capacity. He will do it."

"How can you be so sure? Sir," the voice added hastily.

"Simple. We'll just let him meet her."

"That's all?"

"That's all it will take."

# One

"Alex! The cow got loose again!"

"Telephone, Alex! It's that awful Mr. Rodney again."

"Alex, what are we going to do? Mark didn't come back last night. He must be out in the woods again."

"Alex, help! There's water spraying all over the kitchen! The tape split open again!"

"Alex—"

"All right! Everybody, quiet for a minute!"

Alexandra Logan took a deep breath and pushed her tousled hair back behind one ear. It had been a long time since she'd been able to afford a professional haircut, and it was currently hacked off more or less evenly an inch or so below her ears. It tended to fall forward over her right eye, but it was Aaron's best effort, and she would never hurt his feelings by saying anything.

"All right," she said again. "Sarah, tell Mr. Rodney I'll be right there, then go ahead and feed the chickens. Kenny, turn Cougar loose and follow him. He'll find Daisy. Matt,

would you shut off the water main and tape it up again?
And, Wheezer, would you saddle Cricket for me? I'll go
look for Mark as soon as I get off the phone.''

They scattered in different directions, and Alex smothered a sigh as she walked back into the house. They needed
a new gate that would hold that too-smart bovine, a
plumber to fix pipes that were so old they were nearly
crumbling, a carpenter with more than Matt's rudimentary
skills to fix the chicken coop, the barn, and the roof of the
house, and a miracle to handle everything else that was
falling apart. But the biggest miracle they needed was a way
to get the persistent Mr. Rodney off their backs. She took
another deep breath and picked up the phone.

"Hi, Mr. Rodney. Beautiful day, isn't it?"

"It's the twelfth of the month, Miss Logan."

"And lovely in spite of it," Alex said, her grimace at odds
with her light tone as she listened to the stern voice.

"Miss Logan, I truly must know what you intend to do
about this payment."

"Pay it, of course." So much for hiring a plumber.

"Just when did you have in mind?"

"By the fifteenth. The same terms you gave my father,
naturally."

The pause was barely perceptible, but Alex caught it. She
tightened her grip on the receiver, preparing for battle.

"When the property was your father's, Miss Logan, it
was a working farm."

"It still is. And believe me, I know. I've never worked
harder in my life."

"That is not what I meant. What you are running there
hardly qualifies as a farm."

"Just what is your definition of a farm, Mr. Rodney? I
was under the impression it was a piece of land on which
crops or animals are raised. I think I got that from Web-
ster's dictionary. Do you have a better definition?"

"A true farm is a business, Miss Logan, that engages in
selling its product at a profit, not a refuge for—"

"When was the last time you looked at the agricultural price index, Mr. Rodney? The profit went out of farming years ago. We use everything we raise, and we're virtually independent. We like it that way."

"Well, the people in this neighborhood don't like it. They don't like what you're doing out there, and they don't like the idea of those... people. Only the respect they have for the memory of your parents has kept them from running you off long ago."

Alex felt anger rippling through her, and it was all she could do not to hang up on the man right then.

"I have never missed a payment on this place, Mr. Rodney. And as long as it stays that way, you have no reason and no right to continue this harassment. I don't care what you or anyone else thinks of me or my friends. And if you think I won't fight back, you just try me."

She did hang up then, fiercely. Maybe I should just have the phone disconnected, she thought. We could use the money, and I wouldn't have to talk to idiots like that. Or the sick ones who call and pour out their filthy suggestions.

She felt suddenly weary, and almost eager to go look for Mark. At least she would be away for a while, and any excuse for a peaceful ride up to the high ground was welcome. She turned, then stopped short, a startled gasp rising from her as she came face-to-face with the total stranger standing inside the front door.

"How did you get in here?" And why didn't I hear anything? Why isn't Cougar barking up a storm?

He looked a little dazed, puzzled almost, as he glanced around. "I'm... not sure."

Oh, Lord, Alex thought, not another one. Please, I can't handle another one. We're barely getting by as it is. But as soon as she thought it, she knew there was something wrong with her assessment. For one thing, he was much too young. "Who are you?"

She couldn't help the suspicion in her voice; more than once a ringer had been sent in to try to find some excuse for the local citizens to run her out. But if they thought she was going to believe that this angel-face was—

"Michael. Michael Justice."

Well, at least he knew his name. People had shown up who weren't even sure of that much. Or wouldn't tell her. But he wasn't one of them. She was certain of that. Just as she was certain he was the most beautiful man she'd ever seen.

And, oddly, beautiful was the proper word. Not that he wasn't all male; tall—right at six feet, she guessed—leanly muscled, with a solid jaw and corded tendons in his strong neck. The worn jeans and plain, pale blue T-shirt he wore beneath a battered leather jacket emphasized broad shoulders, a flat belly, and lean, narrow hips. But it was his face that fascinated her.

He was perfect. Every line, every angle, was finely drawn, forehead just high enough, chin just strong enough, nose just narrow and long enough, mouth soft enough to be gentle, yet firm enough to hint at a great strength. His hair was dark, nearly black even in the shaft of sunlight that shot through the window to encircle him. It was cut fairly short and combed neatly back except for a few strands that fell forward over equally dark, perfect brows. His lashes were— inevitably, it seemed—dark, long, and thick. And they surrounded blue eyes that were . . .

It was those eyes, or, rather, the change in them, that derailed her detailed assessment. That dazed look had faded, and he was staring back at her with great interest, interest that told her she had been much too intent on her inspection. She shook herself mentally, telling herself that no matter how perfect he might be, he didn't deserve to have her gaping at him like he'd dropped out of the clouds somewhere.

"Find anything you like?"

Oh, Lord, Alex groaned silently, his voice was perfect, too. Low, vibrant, and with just enough gravel in it to send a shiver up her spine. And blue seemed too tame a word for those eyes, especially now that the puzzled look had gone. They were too vivid, too brilliant, for that mild appellation. They were too alive, as if lit from within rather than by the light streaming through the window.

"If you've ever looked in a mirror, I'm sure you know the answer to that."

She said it simply, with the innate honesty that had more than once been the bane of her existence. He looked startled; then a smile curved his mouth. He had, of course, Alex thought with resignation, a dimple that lit up that perfect face. She forced herself back to the matter at hand before she started another session of cataloguing his assets.

"What I'd really like is an answer. Why are you here?"

The incredible blue eyes rolled heavenward, and Alex got the oddest feeling he was expressing his disgust on a very personal level.

"Apparently," he muttered, "I've been had."

"What?"

"Somebody," he said as his mouth twisted wryly, "knows me too damn well."

He glared upward again, and Alex thought he looked oddly like a little boy purposely tempting fate.

"Waiting for lightning to strike for one little curse?" she asked mildly.

He looked startled, his eyes bright and intent on her. Then he laughed. "Something like that."

"Well, I've got news for you. If we got nailed for every four-letter word that floated around here, there wouldn't be much left."

"Good thing they consider the provocation, then."

"Who?"

"The ones who send the lightning."

"They do?"

"Don't they?"

Her brow furrowed, then cleared. "I guess they must," she said with a laugh, "or we wouldn't be here."

"Sounds like that would suit some people just fine."

She wrinkled her nose. "You heard that, huh?" She couldn't help sighing. "We don't win any popularity contests around here." She suddenly realized he had once again successfully diverted her. "I don't make it a habit of asking a lot of questions, but I like answers to those I do ask." He studied her for a moment; then he glanced around the living room of the small house. He seemed to be waiting for something. Almost absently he raised one hand to finger something that hung around his neck on a golden chain. As he caught it between his thumb and forefinger, his gaze suddenly shot back to her.

"You need some help around here."

"That," she said ruefully, "wouldn't take a genius to see. What does that have to do with why you're here?"

Gold glinted on his chest as he released what looked, she thought in puzzlement, like a set of dog tags. Then he shrugged. "I'm here to help."

"Help...with what?"

"Everything. Anything."

"Look—"

"I'm a decent carpenter, plumber, and electrician. I can muddle my way through most other things."

Hope flared in her, but she beat it down. She knew nothing about this man, she couldn't just—

"It's all right. Really. I know you don't know me, but I'd never hurt you. Or your friends."

Suspicion bit again. Deep. "What do you know about my friends?"

"Just that you're trying to help them. In ways no one else will."

Her eyes narrowed even more as she looked at him. "And how do you know that?"

"I just heard it around, I guess." He saw her doubt and added softly, "I...didn't fight there, but I know what they went through."

Alex didn't know why, but she believed him. She believed that he knew, somehow, of their hell, that he meant them no harm, even while the part of her that had been soured by her recent contacts with her fellow human beings wondered if she wasn't just being fooled by a pretty face.

"Not judging a book by its cover goes both ways, you know."

Her eyes flew to his face. "Was I so obvious?" That honesty again, she thought ruefully.

He smiled, and her heart turned over. "Don't ever try to play poker."

If she had an ounce of brains, she would send him packing, she thought. He was altogether too dangerous to her equilibrium. Then she realized she wouldn't have to send him; he would go on his own when he realized the situation.

"I'm sorry, but we can't afford any help right now."

"Oh?" He looked around again. "You've got a roof, and it looks like you eat fairly regularly. That's all I need."

"The kind of help I need is worth a lot more than just room and board."

"Not to me."

For one of the few times in her life, Alex wavered, unable to decide. She didn't know anything about this man except for his impossible looks and the fact that he seemed to be able to read her far too easily. He could be on the run for all she knew.

"I'm not in trouble or anything. I just need a place to stay."

"The first thing you have to do," she said dryly, "is stop reading my mind."

The dimple flashed again. "Does that mean I can stay?" He didn't give her a chance to say no. "Thanks. And I don't read your mind, just your face. It's very expressive."

She flushed. "If that's a polite way of saying I'm nothing to write home about, don't bother. I already know that."

Something flashed in his blue eyes, dimming for a moment that strange inner glow. It was surprisingly like pain, although for what Alex couldn't guess.

"Don't you ever look in a mirror yourself?" he asked softly.

Her color deepened. "Not if I can help it." She grimaced. "It's bad enough knowing I look like the world's kid sister without reminding myself of it all the time."

"Looking fifteen at twenty-six might be a nuisance, but looking twenty-six at thirty-seven is surely something to look forward to, isn't it?"

She gaped at him, backing up a step. "How did you know how old I am?"

He closed his eyes, letting out a disgusted sigh. "I told you I was tired," he muttered.

When he opened his eyes again Alex was looking at him warily, backing up another step.

"Look, I just—"

He broke off suddenly and started to turn, but not in time to avoid the hulking man who had come in the door behind him. A huge, bearlike arm came around his neck, a snarl issued from somewhere six inches or so above him, and sunlight glinted off the long, deadly blade at his throat.

"Mark!" Alex cried. The big man had moved so quickly that she hadn't even realized what was happening until it was all over. The huge hunting knife hovered much too close to that strong, corded neck. She didn't dare speak yet, knowing Mark's precarious temper when provoked on her behalf. Please, she begged inwardly, just don't move. He won't hurt you if you don't move. He's just trying to protect me.

As if he'd read her once more, Michael went slack, letting the hand that had been clawing at Mark's arm drop to his side. After a moment the snarling subsided, and the big man looked across at Alex.

"Hurt you?"

"No, Mark."

"Sure? You looked scared."

"Just . . . surprised." She managed a credible laugh. "He guessed how old I am. You know how rare that is."

Mark loosened his grip a tiny bit. The knife never wavered.

"Didn't hurt you?"

"No. In fact, he came to help."

The grip tightened again. "Help what?"

"Fix things. The gate maybe, and even the pipes. Isn't that right?"

Slowly, tentatively, eyes never leaving the gleaming blade at his throat, Michael nodded. The grip relaxed again.

"Too pretty to be much good."

"And you're too big to be going around scaring the daylights out of people," she said sternly. The knife finally dropped, and Mark stepped back.

"Thought he hurt you."

"I know. It's all right. But you should apologize to Mr. Justice."

The snarl rose again, but it ended in a gruff, "Sorry."

He got a wary nod in return.

"Where were you, Mark? We were worried."

"Walkin'."

"All night?"

"Sat. Watched the stars, listened to the night."

"I understand, Mark. I love to do that, too. But remember what you promised me?"

The huge, bearded man looked incredibly sheepish. "Leave note." Alex nodded. "Forgot." She waited, not speaking. The big man blushed. "Sorry."

She went to him then, throwing her arms around him in as much of a hug as she could manage, given that he towered at least a foot over her own five foot six. Huge arms encircled her with a gentle care that was amazing in a man so strong. Yet it was awkward, as if an unfamiliar action. And what could be seen of his face above the bushy beard was flaming.

"It's okay, Mark. Just remember next time, okay? You've got people who worry about you now."

"Okay."

"Will you go out to the barn? I won't need Cricket saddled after all."

The bearded head bobbed up and down; then the big man turned to go. At the last second he looked back over his shoulder, fixing the man he'd just had in a death grip with a warning look.

"You hurt her, you got big trouble. We take care of her. Die for her, if we have to. Or kill for her."

"I believe you," Michael said softly. It seemed to appease the big man, and he went out the door.

When he looked back at her, Michael had to smother a smile. She was glaring at him, fists clenched, waiting. He didn't need to read her mind; she looked like a tigress defending her cub. As he'd said, her face was very expressive.

"He's . . . very special, isn't he?"

"Yes," she said flatly, searching his face for any sign of sarcasm. She found none.

"I'm glad he's your friend." A smile tugged at one corner of his mouth. "And I'm sure he meant every word he said."

Alex felt the tension drain out of her; she couldn't seem to hang on to her wariness or her doubts when he turned those uncanny eyes on her.

"Mark . . . exaggerates sometimes."

"Everyone does, sometimes. But I don't think he was, not about that." He looked at her steadily. "How many live here? Six?"

She answered before she thought to wonder how he had come so close. She supposed he'd heard about it wherever he'd heard that she needed help.

"Seven, at the moment."

He looked at the small house. "You have room for me?"

"We converted one of the barns into a bunkhouse of sorts. The guys stay there. But you can't."

"I can't?"

"They're very...wary of strangers. Even if you were one of them, you'd have to stay here for a couple of weeks, until they decided if they trusted you or not."

"And since I'm not...one of them?"

"It will take even longer. Especially for you."

"Why especially?"

"Well," she said, the corners of her mouth twitching, "you *are* awfully pretty."

He stared at her, grinned, then burst into delighted laughter. The sound washed over her, soothing and invigorating at the same time. It was a sound too rarely heard around here to be taken for granted, and just for a moment she let herself luxuriate in it, let a wide smile that was a little lopsided from lack of use spread across her face.

"Lady," he finally choked out, "if they can stand you being around, I'm sure not going to bother them."

Her smile disappeared. "You don't have to do that. I already said you could stay."

"Do what?"

"We're very careful about the truth around here. That's something you'd better learn."

"Exactly what did I do," he asked carefully, "that brought this on?"

"The people here have no patience with any kind of phoniness, especially false flattery. And that includes me."

"False fla—" He broke off, staring at her. "You mean what I said about you?"

"I know what I look like, Mr. Justice."

"You may look, but I don't think you see."

"Cryptic comments don't go over well here, either."

"You really don't know how lovely you are, do you?"

Her cheeks flamed, and hurt tinged her voice. "If you insist on mocking me, you can leave now."

That oddly pained look flickered in his eyes again. "I'm sorry. I didn't mean that at all." He reached out one hand to lightly touch her arm.

Alex stared at him. The moment his warm fingers had brushed her skin, her embarrassment, her hurt, had vanished. She was filled instead with a sense of calm and peace such as she'd never known.

"I would never try to hurt you," he promised solemnly.

"I . . . I know."

That was ridiculous, Alex thought. How could she know that?

There was a thump at the back of the house, and an odd clattering across the bare wood floor. His eyes flicked in that direction, then back to Alex's face; she was unperturbed. A familiar sound, then. In a moment he saw why.

The dog that gamboled into the room was the size of a small pony. Shaggy, with a huge head and a medium length coat of several shades of brown and tan, he looked of no particular breed, but it was doubtful that anyone would ever hold it against him. The huge animal carefully stationed himself in front of Alex and looked at the room's other occupant suspiciously. Michael looked back wryly.

"What's Cricket, a Clydesdale?"

It took her a moment to realize what he meant. Then she smiled as she realized that, so far, everything he'd seen here had been a little on the large side. The smile became a chuckle, then a laugh. A laugh she hadn't used in so long it felt strange. Even the dog looked askance at her, his half-floppy ears cocked attentively at the unusual sound.

"This," she said through the lingering remnants of her laughter, "is Cougar."

"After the color, the size, or the temperament?"

The laughter came more easily this time. "None of the above. I found him over near Cougar Dam. He'd been hit by a car, and they just left him."

"Oh." He knelt down until he was level with the massive head. The dog stretched out his nose as far as he could without leaving Alex's side. Michael didn't move. Finally the dog did, taking one hesitant step. Then he looked back over his shaggy shoulder at Alex.

"It's okay," she said softly.

The wet nose found his hand then. The moment they touched, the dog went suddenly still; even the tentative wag of the plumed tail stopped. The huge, soulful eyes were fastened on Michael's face, staring intently. Then he spoke to the animal, low and rough.

"Yes."

It was all he said, but the effect was electrifying. An odd sound, half bark, half howl, rose from Cougar's throat as Alex watched the remarkable reaction. She knew the sound as the animal's most joyous greeting, and she'd never heard it directed at anyone but herself before.

When Michael stood up again, she was staring at him.

"I...he's never reacted like that to a stranger before. He's usually very wary."

"And protective? Like Mark?"

Her cheeks pinkened slightly. "Yes."

"I hope you take him with you when you go anywhere."

"Yes." She smiled a little ruefully. "Don't laugh, but I traded my little car for a pickup just so he can ride along. It makes me feel better if I have to go into town."

"I wouldn't laugh." He grinned. "I wouldn't laugh at anybody with a dog that size at their beck and call. And I would never laugh at you."

The sudden seriousness of his tone brought the color back to her cheeks. "I...sometimes I'm a little sensitive."

He started to say something, then stopped.

"I'll show you where you can stay," she said hastily. "Are your things outside?"

"No. They're right here."

He turned around and picked up a large leather knapsack that was as battered as the jacket he wore. Alex's brows furrowed; she hadn't noticed the bag there before. But it had been halfway behind the open front door, so she supposed she could have missed it. She was used to men arriving here with no more than they could carry, so she didn't comment on the apparent meagerness of his possessions.

"The kitchen's in there," she said, gesturing toward a big room visible through an arched passageway. "And the dining room. We tore out a wall to get a table in there big enough for all of us. We usually eat together."

He only nodded. She led him down a narrow hall toward the back of the house, past another door, and to the room at the end. It was small, but it had several large, screened windows that looked out on an expanse of green pasture, making it seem much more spacious. There were inexpensive but effective bamboo shades rolled up at the top of each one.

"It's not much," she began, but he shook his head.

"It's fine. Perfect. I like the windows."

He set the knapsack down on the narrow bed that sat beneath the windows. He looked out at the pasture, noting that the fence, although sturdy enough, badly needed some paint. He could see where repairs had been made and guessed that the money had stretched far enough for essentials, but not for the luxury of paint.

"The bathroom's right down the hall, the first door we passed," she told him. "Feel free. Mine's at the other end of the house."

He looked back over his shoulder at her and nodded. She glanced at her watch.

"Lunch is at eleven. We get started early around here, so we eat early. I'll introduce you to everyone then."

He nodded again.

"Then I'll show you around, if you like."

"I would. Thanks."

She sensed his sudden reserve and backed hastily to the door of the small room. "I'll let you get settled, then."

"Thank you. At lunch you can tell me where you want me to start."

"All right."

"Thanks, Alex."

She didn't see him cross the room after she'd gone, or stand in the doorway as he listened to her footsteps fade away; she was too busy trying to remember when she'd told him her name.

Only when he heard the front door open, then close after her, did Michael close his own door and go back to sit on the edge of the bed. He slipped off the leather jacket and tossed it aside.

Great, he muttered silently. I have most definitely been had. Set up for a fall. Shuffled, shaken, and rolled, coming up in front of a sassy little nose with a sprinkling of freckles, and a pair of green eyes that could convince anybody that the world is really a beautiful place if you look hard enough.

He reached up and tugged the gold chain over his head. For a moment he just sat there, staring at the two tags that dangled from the necklace. One bore only his name and a date in an ornate script, the other a stylized image of a dragon. The boss, he'd decided when he'd first seen it, had a warped sense of humor.

At last his hand wrapped around the two tags. Slowly his eyes closed.

*Yes, Michael.*

Uh-uh. I want the boss.

*Michael—*

You heard me. I've had one too many fast ones pulled on me. I want the boss.

*We understand you're upset. And we don't blame you. But surely you can understand why we had to do it. You know how crazy things have been, Michael. Michael? Michael, we know you're there. Really, Michael! Such a temper! Oh, all right.*

That's better.

His hand tightened around the golden tags.

*You rang?*

Cute. Just like this little stunt you pulled.

*Me?*

Save it. It had your fingerprints all over it.

*We don't have fingerprints.*

Quit tap dancing.

*We don't have feet, either. Oh, all right, Michael. You're quite right, it was rather underhanded of me.*

I thought you didn't have hands?

*I'm glad to see you've regained your sense of humor.*

I haven't. I was just checking to see what parts I could imagine slicing off.

*Michael, really!*

You promised. You guys aren't supposed to break promises.

*It wasn't broken. Merely... postponed.*

For just a second he let his weariness seep through.

*I'm truly sorry, Michael. We have overworked you tremendously, I know. But if you weren't so efficient—*

Flattery doesn't become you.

*No, I suppose not. It is true, however. But we do realize you're not at your peak right now. So we've arranged a little help. You won't need clearance for the basics. If you need anything extra, just ask.*

Is that your subtle way of letting me know there's no way out of this?

*Do you really want out, Michael? Now that you've met her?*

Now *that* is sneaky! You know I'm a sucker for an innocent against the world.

*Yes. That's why you're so good at this. And that, Michael, is not flattery.*

He sighed, then accepted it.

All right. But this is it.

*I understand.*

I'm so tired I nearly blew this already. I've never met a woman less impressed with her own beauty. And you were no help, dumping me in here without a clue.

*I know.*

After this, I'm through. For a *long* time.

*Thank you, Michael.*

Right. You have the details for me?

*Yes. Whenever you're ready.*

One more thing. Is she really as ... special as she seems?

A pause. Then, *Yes, she is.*

That's what I got from Cougar. She sat up with him for four nights in a row, coaxing him to live.

*Yes. She would. And she has done much more for the people she has helped.*

I know. I picked it up from Mark. It was a little confused, because he was so angry and also scared for her, but he meant it when he said he'd die for her. Or kill for her.

*We must see that he is never confronted with that necessity. He's been hurt too much already. He'll be protected, as well.*

All right. I'm ready when you are.

*In thirty seconds, then. I wish you good luck, Michael.*

You *wish* me? You guys make the luck, remember? You'd damn well better make sure of it.

*Michael, your language. I've been meaning to talk to you about that.*

But you've been too busy bouncing me around, haven't you? Just send the stuff, will you?

He could have sworn, as he swung his feet up and lay back on the narrow bed, waiting for the flood of communication, that he heard a chuckle.

# Two
---

"And this is Cricket. He's my oldest friend, aren't you, love?" Alex crooned, patting the strong neck.

Michael looked at the flashy black-and-white pinto that had danced eagerly to the fence the moment she whistled. He was marked like a pristine white horse that had had glistening black paint poured over his back; the effect was dramatic.

"Oldest friend? How long have you had him?" he asked, waiting quietly while the horse eyed him warily.

"Since he was a foal. He's almost eleven now."

Michael held out a hand, and the black nose snuffled it as the black-and-white head bobbed. Only then did he lay a hand on the animal's neck. Images, clear and vivid, rippled through the connection. Alex, a fifteen-year-old pixie in fiery red pigtails, so unlike the rich auburn of her hair now, hugging the newborn colt in delight. And a devastated, weeping Alex, huddled in a pile of straw as the tiny animal nudged her urgently. And, later, an older Alex, shadows haunting her eyes, mounting the three-year-old horse for a long, lonely ride into the forested hills.

He knew the meaning behind each of those images now, and he sent the loving animal a quick, reassuring message. *I'm here to help her. I promise. Things will change for her now.*

Alex stared as the paint horse let out an exultant whinny.

"You certainly seem to have a way with animals," she observed, a little warily.

"I give them enough credit," he said simply, "and they know it." With a little help.

She studied him for a moment. "Too bad it doesn't work on people."

He shrugged. It would, if he wanted to use it, but he preferred not to. But he knew what she meant; lunch had been, if not quite unpleasant, strained. He didn't blame the men at the big table. He was the newcomer, the intruder, and above all the one who had shared none of the horrors that had brought them here to this refuge Alex provided.

"You seem awfully calm about it," she said.

He shrugged again. "I didn't expect a rousing welcome, if that's what you mean. I know I'll have to earn a place here with them." He turned around, leaning his back against the fence. "And with you."

One brow, curved into a delicate arc he knew she would deny was beautiful, rose questioningly. His heart twisted inside him. Any other woman would have immediately read some kind of personal invitation into his words; this one was so uncertain of her own appeal that the possibility never occurred to her. He felt something tug, tighten, deep inside, an odd sensation that he couldn't remember ever having felt before. She was so beautiful, he thought, and she didn't see it. He would have to work on that. But for now, he merely went on quietly.

"You still don't trust me completely, either."

He didn't seem upset by it, so Alex didn't bother to deny it. She even admitted to herself that part of her distrust stemmed from his amazing looks. She couldn't quite believe that a man so perfect could possibly be as open and sensitive as he seemed. He should be a snob, arrogant and utterly conceited. He'd no doubt had people—women, she told herself in a determined effort to blunt her unexpected response—cater to him all his life, and it should have shown.

Yet she could find no sign of it. When he looked at her with those glowing blue eyes, she felt odd inside, as if he'd scoured her soul down to its very essence with his gaze. Yet at the same time she felt comforted, as if, just for that moment in time, she could put aside the problems that beset her, as if just for that moment she could rest. And oh, how she would love to rest, just for a while.

"You can trust me, Alex. I'm only here to help. Let me carry some of the burden for a while."

She stared at him, green eyes wide, and he knew he'd once again skated a little too close to the edge with her.

"So tell me, who does what around here?" he asked quickly. "I don't want to compound my problems by stepping on anyone's toes."

It had to be coincidence, Alex thought. Or perhaps she really was such a silly little fool that her every thought showed in her face. She sighed, then set herself to answering him.

"Well, Matt's our fledgling carpenter. He's got the desire and the enthusiasm, but he's a little short on experience. He'd only just begun when he got called up, and he never went back to it. Steven was a medic, so he's our first line of defense when it comes to cuts and bruises. Wheezer works with the animals—"

"Let me guess . . . he's allergic to them? They make him wheeze?"

She nodded. "Dr. Swan gave him some medicine that controls it, but the name had already stuck by then."

"Dr. Swan?" He already knew who the man was, but he wanted to hear her reaction.

"He's the doctor at the clinic in town. And one of the few who doesn't want us all ridden out on a rail."

"Why?"

"He lost his son in Nam. He couldn't help him, so . . ."

Michael nodded. "And you, Alex? Why do you do it?"

She shrugged. "It needs to be done." She continued her discourse briskly. "Now Kenny, he grew up on a small farm in Nebraska. Different kind of country, but the principle's the same, he says. So he directs most of the actual planting and real farm work. Sarah's his wife, and I'd be lost without her. She is, as you probably noticed, a great cook."

He smiled. "Yes."

"Aaron helps me with the paperwork and does his best at haircuts," she went on dryly, tugging at her own thick mop.

He reached out and touched the thick section that tended to flop in front of her eye. "All you need is a little trim here in front. Some bangs, maybe. I like your hair," he added carefully. She couldn't argue with what he liked, could she? "I like the way it lights up in the sun, all red and alive."

"Ol' carrot top, that's me," Alex muttered, trying to shake off the odd feeling his touch gave her.

"Maybe once, when you were younger. But not now, Alex. Your hair looks like all the colors of warmth. Brown, bronze, and a splash of fire."

Alex automatically opened her mouth to protest his compliment but found herself saying instead, "That was . . . rather poetic."

"It's hard to talk of the beauty in the world without sounding that way. Now," he said quickly, "don't go all prickly on me. I just like the color of your hair, all right?"

He drew back his hand, and Alex turned to face the fence, leaning on the top rail for the support she suddenly seemed to need.

"What about Rick?" he asked, as if the interlude had never occurred.

"We don't know much about him. He's only been here three weeks or so. Just moved to the bunkhouse last week.

He hasn't talked much, and, as you see, we don't pry. One of the guys who left here last year sent him up from Los Angeles."

"One of your successes?"

"I suppose. He's got a good job now and is trying to put his family back together."

"You're doing a good thing here, Alex."

"Not according to the city fathers," she said, a trace of bitterness in her voice.

"Do you really care what they think?"

"Only because it affects the guys. They know what the people think, that they half expect them to go off on some horrible rampage. If it were me, I'd be half tempted to do it just because I knew they expected it."

"Make it a self-fulfilling prophecy?"

"Something like that," she admitted a little sheepishly. Then the touch of acidity returned. "They see all that crap on television and in the movies, and they think that anybody who was in that stinking war came back a menace to society. I don't blame a lot of guys for giving up and just becoming what everybody thought they were in the first place."

"It was ugly," Michael said softly. "All wars are. But the one they had to fight when they came home was a different kind of ugly. And in many ways worse. In Vietnam, it was their bodies and their spirits that were killed or maimed. Here it was their souls, because this was home, this was the place they'd dreamed of coming back to. It was supposed to be safe."

"And it turned out to be just a different kind of hell."

"Except," Michael said softly, looking around, "for a few small miracles wrought by some very special people." His eyes came back to her face. "You built this for them, Alex. The sanctuary they should have had."

"It's not enough," she whispered.

"You built it, and you've kept it going for eight years. That's a hell of a lot to expect from an eighteen-year-old girl."

Her stunned look told him that he was walking the edge again, told him that only now was she realizing that she had poured out things to him that she rarely told anyone. "How...how do you know all this?"

"I just put some bits and pieces together." He changed the subject swiftly. "Where do you want me to start?"

She accepted the switch gratefully. "How good a plumber are you? Can you work miracles?"

His mouth twitched. "Give me a try."

"It'll take one," she said grimly, leading the way back to the house. "These pipes are as old as the house, and it's beginning to show. And replacing them is a long way in the financial future."

"They might just surprise you and hold out a little longer—with some help," he said.

"My luck," she said sourly, "isn't that good."

"Luck," he said with an upward glance, "can change."


"What about this guy, Alex?"

Aaron was looking at her worriedly, glancing out the window to where Michael was tugging chicken wire over the new frame he'd built. He'd done it in one morning, Alex thought in amazement, using the wood from the old coop, most of which she would have sworn was too rotten to be reused. That was why she hadn't asked Matt to try to fix it, knowing they couldn't afford any new lumber. The last of what they owned had gone to repair the fence Cricket had broken down the night they'd had the prowler.

"I mean," Aaron said, "are you sure about him?"

She turned to look at the sandy-haired man whose eyes were blurred behind thick glasses. "As sure as I was about you when you first came here."

He had the grace to blush. "Oops."

"You guys have been pretty hard on him, Aaron. And he's never complained, just takes it and keeps going. And he's accomplished more in a week than we have in a month."

"I guess we have been riding him a bit."

"A bit?"

"Okay, a lot."

"Still think he's nothing but a pretty face?"

Aaron adjusted his glasses, avoiding her gaze. "Been that transparent, has it?"

"Don't feel bad. It was my first reaction too. But now I'm very glad he's here. He managed to fix that leak with that piece of pipe he found God knows where, he found those shingles up in the attic that I didn't even know were there and fixed the roof, not to mention repairing that old ladder of ours so it's usable. He's done a hundred little things none of us have had the time or the talent for, and now he's almost done with the chicken coop."

"You sure that's . . . all you're glad about?"

"Aaron, don't talk in circles. What are you saying?"

"Just that . . . some of the guys, we were talking. He is a good looking guy, and he *is* about your age. We thought that maybe . . ."

"Maybe what?"

"Well, you know. That you might be glad he was here for other reasons."

"Other reasons? What are you getting at?"

Aaron looked horribly embarrassed, and his cheeks were red as he took off his glasses and wiped them laboriously on his shirttail.

"You've been here with us a long time, Alex. Since you were just a kid."

"It's where I wanted to be."

Her voice was soothing. Aaron had been here since the beginning. He'd been Andrew's best friend "in country," and when he'd shown up one day just before Andrew's death, he'd stayed. At first to help, and then, he later admitted, to get what he needed himself: peace and a sense of purpose.

"We know that. But you're missing out on a life of your own, Alex, stuck out here with a bunch of guys practically old enough to be your father."

She laughed. "Matt's the oldest, and he's only forty-eight. That hardly puts any of you in the geriatric category."

"But you need to see people your own age."

"Let me worry about that, will you?"

Aaron's eyes flicked to the window again. "Just be careful, will you? We don't know much about him."

"Aaron," she said, following the direction of his glance, "what on earth would make you think that a man like him would look twice at someone like me?"

"Don't be so hard on yourself. If you ever took any time for yourself instead of spending it all on us—"

"Relax, Aaron. I'm quite resigned to being a perennial little sister. It doesn't bother me anymore."

But it did, she thought. Or seemed to lately. Why else was she so—what had Michael called it?—prickly about the casual compliments he'd given her? She used to just slough off things like that as the meaningless patter that seemed endemic to the male of the species when confronted with a female, no matter what she looked like. So why was she reacting this way now? Was she getting restless? Or was it simply because of the source of those compliments?

She smothered a little sigh. Of course it was, she thought as she stared out the window at him. What woman alive could come in contact with a man like Michael Justice and not react?

Although she'd actually seen very little of him since that first day; he'd been up and out at dawn, frequently not finishing whatever chores he'd set for himself until the evening meal.

Meals, she thought ruefully, that were still an ordeal. Instead of the usual good-natured teasing, silence reigned, the only conversation being an occasional gibe at Michael, generally preceded by a derisive, "Hey, pretty boy." Even a seat on one of the long benches at the table was surrendered to him grudgingly, with barely veiled hostility.

He never reacted, never showed the slightest sign that they were getting to him, while Alex found it all she could do not to get up and rap a couple of stubborn heads together. Only Rick, as usual, stayed silent, and only Mark showed him any kind of politeness, apparently having decided that Alex's acceptance was good enough for him.

She watched him as he nailed down the wire he'd mended and stretched over the frame. He moved so smoothly, his arm coming down in a graceful arc time after time as he swung the hammer. She watched his arm flex beneath the sleeve of his T-shirt, watched the cloth stretch tight as his muscles bunched.

His hair was falling forward over his forehead, and she wondered what it would feel like to brush it back. It would feel like silk, she thought, heavy dark silk. She would brush it back, he would look up at her with those incredible blue eyes, and—

And she would be humiliated out of her mind. He would be embarrassed, and she would slink off and look for a hole to hide in. She could just guess what he would be thinking: All I did was be nice to the girl. She must be really starved for attention. How could she think I would really be interested in someone who looks like a fifteen-year-old tomboy?

Suddenly Michael froze, his arm dropping to his side in midstroke. His head came up, and he looked back over his shoulder. Alex drew back instinctively, even though she knew he couldn't possibly see her from there.

It would serve you right if he could, she scolded herself severely. Wouldn't he just laugh his head off to know the little country girl had been drooling over him?

No, she thought with a sudden certainty she couldn't explain, he wouldn't laugh. He'd said he never would, and she believed him. But he would probably feel sorry for her, and somehow that was much, much worse.

So get yourself together, girl. Just because he happens to be gorgeous and, as Aaron said, closer to your age, is no reason to treat him any differently than any of the other men here. And you'd do well to remember that.

And so, she thought suddenly, would the rest of them. So when the others were gathered around the table that night while Michael was still outside washing up, she found herself trying to make them see it.

"I think," she said casually as she set a plate of biscuits on the table, "that we should all go in and apologize to the whole town at the meeting this month."

"What?"

Seven voices in unison made a powerful noise, she thought wryly. "I just mean that you can't really blame the people for being difficult. I mean, they only know what they see on the surface. What else do they have to judge by?"

"What kind of talk is that? And from you, Alex!" Hurt and indignation were etched on Wheezer's face.

Alex shrugged elaborately. "Well, it's obvious you've all come around to their way of thinking, so I thought now that you're in agreement—"

"Come around to what?" Steve asked angrily, tugging at his thick moustache as he always did when perturbed. "And apologize for what? For being ourselves? For not denying what we are? If they can't see past the surface, it's their problem! And you're the one who taught us that, Alex!"

"Not well enough, apparently."

"What do you mean?" Kenny spoke this time, puzzlement in his voice and hurt in his innocent, farm-boy face.

"Apparently you think it only goes one way. That only you deserve that effort to see past the surface."

"Of course we don't," Matt began protestingly. "We know that—"

"Uh-oh."

Aaron's voice was quiet, but it stopped them all dead.

"Uh-oh what?"

"I think she's got us, boys." His eyes flickered to the porch, where the sound of water at the tap they used for washing up had stopped. "Think about it."

There was, Alex noticed with satisfaction, more than one sheepish look around the table. Her point made, she said no more, just sat down at her place at the head of the table, the place she took at their tacit insistence; whenever she came to sit down, it was the only place left.

There was a moment of silence as Michael came in. Eight pairs of eyes fastened on him, and Alex thought she caught the slightest hint of weariness in those sky blue eyes. She didn't blame him, she thought. He'd been working so hard, and then to have to face this every night... She wondered that he didn't just take his meal and disappear somewhere to eat in peace. Except, she thought, that there wasn't an ounce of quit in him.

She saw his lips tighten for just a second, then saw him let out a short, compressed breath. Then he looked away, tossing the towel he'd used in the laundry basket by the door before he started toward the table. He stopped short, startled, when Kenny slid over on one bench.

"There's room here," he said.

Michael's eyes flicked to Alex, and she had that odd feeling again, as if he could read everything that had happened in the room in her eyes. Slowly he took the proffered seat, eyeing them all a little warily.

"Have a biscuit," Steve said gruffly, holding out the plate. And without a word Matt handed him the glass of ice water he'd just poured and began to pour another for himself.

Michael stared at the glass suspiciously. "Is it laced with anything interesting?"

The sheepish looks reappeared, except for Mark, who, from his seat to Alex's right, guffawed suddenly. All eyes turned to him.

"Don't blame him. Been treating him like they treat us."

"Yes," Aaron said. "Yes, we have. And for that we owe you an apology."

Michael seemed stunned. "I... thank you."

"Thank Alex. She made us see it."

His eyes went back to her, searching her face. She blushed and wanted to look away, but she couldn't seem to tear her eyes away from his. After a moment he smiled, as if he'd found what he'd been looking for.

"Thank you," he said softly, and the weariness she'd seen vanished, as if he'd gotten a sudden burst of energy.

Michael settled back as a steady rain of chatter began around the table, a return of what was clearly their normal demeanor. Sarah arrived with a steaming plate of potatoes and pork chops, then took a seat next to her husband.

While Kenny talked about the apple crop and Wheezer sighed over a milking machine they couldn't afford, Michael just sat quietly and savored the unexpected jolt of strength he'd gotten. A small miracle had occurred here, and he'd had absolutely nothing to do with it. It had been Alex who had done it, and with no help other than her own generous heart.

She was indeed as special as she seemed, he thought. That must explain it, this odd, warm feeling he got inside whenever he looked at her. It was a sensation he'd never felt before, and he didn't quite know what to make of it. It unsettled him, and he wasn't used to being unsettled.

"—thanks to Michael."

Alex's voice yanked him back to the present. "I'm sorry. What?"

"I was just saying that you've saved us the money we set aside for the roof and the plumbing. And the lumber for a new coop. We'll actually have something left after I make the payment on the farm this month."

"Oh. Good." He glanced around the table. "I gather everybody kicks in for that?"

"We all have something coming in from the government," Matt said with a grimace, running a hand through thick brown hair flecked with gray. "Deserving veterans that we are."

"We give half of whatever we get to Alex for the payments on the place," Steve explained.

"Oh. I... wish I could help, but—"

"Don't be silly," Alex said quickly. "Didn't I just say that thanks to you we've even got money left? We're just trying to figure out how to spend it. There's not enough for everything, but we thought maybe a new gate—"

"I'm going to fix that tomorrow. It just needs new hinges and a latch that Daisy can't get at. I found some hinges in the toolshed, and I can make the latch."

"I don't remember seeing any hinges in there," Matt said.

"I found 'em in a corner on the floor," Michael answered easily.

"Oh. Well, maybe we can get the stove fixed for Sarah. You know what a pain that thing is, but we haven't been able to afford to have someone come—"

"We don't need to," Sarah interrupted with a smile at Michael. "Michael fixed it this morning. It works fine now. Even that fourth burner that never worked. I think we should get Mark's radio fixed. You know how much he misses listening to his music."

Mark's bearded head came up, and he reached into his jacket pocket and drew out a small portable radio. With a grin he turned a knob and the unmistakable beat of a sixties rock tune filled the room. He grinned as he turned it off.

"Michael," he said simply.

The expressions around the table changed from sheepish to ashamed.

"I feel," Kenny said, "like I've been kicking Lassie."

"Lassie," Michael said composedly, "would have bitten you long ago."

They stared at him, wide-eyed, but when they caught the glint of humor in his eyes, they all burst out laughing. And from that moment on, all enmity was forgotten, and when the friendly heckling began again, he was a victim as much as any of them. Only Rick failed to join in and was heard to mutter, "Still too damned pretty," as he got up to leave. Alex's voice stopped him.

"Rick?"

"What?"

"Your plate?"

He glared at her, but he picked up his dirty dishes and carried them to the kitchen. Michael watched him go, his eyes narrowed. Rick was an angry man, but was he angry enough to be behind the trouble here?

"Teach him manners, if you want," Mark said to Alex, his eyes narrowing as he watched the man go.

"No. Not yet, anyway. We give everybody a month to settle in, remember?" Her eyes flicked to Michael, and she was thinking of how they'd crammed all the testing, the "feeling out" they usually did with a newcomer into such a short period of time. "Sometimes we even give it to them in a week."

Michael grinned at her, and Alex congratulated herself for not showing what that flashing dimple did to her silly insides. The rest of them laughed, still a little abashed, and she knew that meals would be back to normal now. For everyone, that was, but her. Now she had nothing left to worry about except her own stupid reactions to his presence.

"We still haven't decided about the money," she said hastily.

"Maybe we should just save it," Sarah said. "For the next thing that falls apart."

"Maybe we should pay Michael," Steve said seriously.

"That's an idea!" Alex said with enthusiasm, and everyone at the table chimed in in agreement.

"Fine," Michael said. "Consider it my contribution to the cause, then."

"But that puts us right back to square one," Aaron said. "Besides, you've more than earned it. And all of us have something left after we kick in our share, so you should, too."

"Something to spend any way I want, you mean?"

They nodded.

"Okay. Then I want to spend it to send Alex on a vacation."

"What?" It was a startled yelp as she stared at him.

"I know you don't know anything about them," Michael said with mock innocence, "but that's when you go away and let other people take care of you for a change. Relax, go to a movie, have a nice dinner out, room service for breakfast, have your hair done, go shopping—"

"I can't do that!"

"I think it's a great idea," Sarah enthused.

"Me too," Steve agreed. "To some place away from here, where you can just have a good time and not worry."

"But we need that money—"

"We agreed to give it to Michael, remember?" Wheezer said.

"And I told you how I'm going to spend it."

"Doesn't look like you have much choice," Aaron put in with a grin. "There's enough left for a nice weekend in Eugene, or maybe even Portland. What do you say? A movie or a play, a little champagne brunch on Sunday morning?"

"I . . . I can't!"

"Just because you never have?" Matt said. "You work and work, Alex, right alongside us. But at least we take some time off on the weekends. For you, that's just when you start wrestling with the rest of our problems. The bills, the paperwork, fighting with the government when they mess up our checks, deciding what gets done now and what gets put off. You need a break, kid."

"I don't mind. And that's why I can't possibly—"

"Yes, you can." Kenny interrupted. "Matt's right. You do all the things we don't want to do, don't want to bother with. You just do them and do them and never complain. And we—" he looked around at the others "—we never thank you enough."

"Work too damn hard," Mark put in gruffly.

"And most of all," Sarah added softly, "you face those awful people, the ones who hate us and want us to leave. And we let you."

"It's just...easier for me. I know them. I can handle them."

"Why?"

She looked startled by Michael's quiet question.

"I...because they know me, too, I guess. And they knew my parents. It makes it a little harder for them to be...nasty."

"I meant, why do you do it?"

"Why...?"

"Why do you do it at all? Why do you push yourself so hard? It sure isn't for the money, is it?"

"Of course not."

"It's because it makes you feel good, isn't it? Makes you feel like you're contributing, helping?"

"I suppose so—"

"Then quit being so selfish."

She heard the startled movements of the others, but they didn't register as she gaped at him. "What?"

"You think you're the only one who likes feeling good? You want to keep it all to yourself? Let somebody else feel good for a change. Let somebody else do something for you and feel good about it."

Steve laughed suddenly. "All right! Got you, Alex!"

She looked around at all the faces that were grinning at her from around the table. She opened her mouth to speak but couldn't think of a thing to say.

"Nice work, Mike," Matt put in, any lingering doubts about this newcomer to their midst erased now.

"I can't," Alex murmured, a little stunned at how things had been turned around on her. "There's too much to do."

"You can, moppet," Steve said. "We'll manage."

"But I'd feel so...guilty!"

"Just think how guilty you'll feel if you disappoint us," Aaron said, winking at Michael in thanks for finding the only argument that would work with her.

"But..."

"Let somebody do something for you for a change," Michael said softly.

Alex turned her head to look at him. The glowing warmth of his eyes seemed to reach out and envelop her, coaxing her, cajoling her.

"I'll...think about it."

"Don't think. Just do it. This weekend."

"Michael, I can't."

"You pack, you get in the truck, you go. Easy."

"But I can't. My truck needs—"

"A new rotor. Plugs. Valves adjusted. I know. I did it yesterday."

She stared at him. "When did you have ti—"

"It didn't take long. That's your last excuse, Alex."

She couldn't fight him anymore. The power of those glowing blue eyes was too much, the strength in them so much more than hers. As if he were willing her to do it, she slowly nodded.

Later, as she lay in bed, she wondered how it had all happened, how she had managed to let herself get maneuvered into this. The image of all of them, smiling at her from around the table, told her how true Michael's words had been; how could she deny them the pleasure this simple thing seemed to give them?

It was difficult for her; taking was not something she was used to. But they were so intent on it, so determined to carry out this idea Michael had come up with, that she didn't have the heart to say no. And deep inside her, a little kernel of anticipation began to grow.

Two days, free of the burdens that were sometimes so hard, even when carried willingly. Two days out of eight years, that wasn't so much, was it? Two days, just for herself? To be at no one's beck and call, to do as she pleased, relieved of the constant demands on her time and energy?

"Thank you, Michael," she whispered into the darkness, wondering how he'd known how badly she needed this when she hadn't even known it herself. That he'd known and had acted to fulfill that need touched her deeply. And gave rise to thoughts she didn't dare let form, didn't dare dwell upon.

She snuggled into her pillow, sleep beginning to creep in despite the image that lingered in her mind, an image of eyes so searingly blue it was like looking at the sky on a perfect summer day. Two whole days, she thought drowsily. She could—

The sharp jangle of the phone jarred her awake, and she reached for the receiver automatically, before she stopped to think.

"Hello?"

"You haven't learned your lesson yet, have you, bitch? Well, you will. And you'll be sorry you didn't get out when you had the chance. Before someone got hurt."

# Three

Michael came awake abruptly, sitting bolt upright in the narrow bed. Fear rippled over him in waves, a fear barely touched with anger. He let his senses stretch, much as a wolf scenting the breeze, and in a moment he had it.

"Alex."

It came out on a harsh breath, and he rolled out of bed and came to his feet in one smooth motion. He grabbed his jeans and yanked them on, then ran barefoot down the hall to the room he'd never seen but knew was hers.

She was sitting up in the big four-poster bed, her hand cramped tightly around the telephone receiver. She was shaking, staring at the instrument as if she'd mistakenly grabbed a snake and now didn't dare let go for fear of being bitten.

"Alex."

He was across the room in one long stride. He sat on the edge of the bed and pried the phone from her fingers. He flipped on the bedside light, its dim bulb casting only a faint glow onto the bed.

"I . . . thought it . . . was over. . . ."

Her teeth were chattering, much more than the slight chill of the room warranted. He felt an odd tightness inside at the sight of her in the big bed, a reaction he didn't understand at all. He pushed it aside; he had to concentrate on the fear that was making her shiver. He hung up the phone and turned back to her.

"What, Alex? You thought what was over?"

"I thought he'd . . . given up. He hadn't called. Not for weeks."

"Who?"

"I don't know. He disguises his voice."

"Alex, what did he say? Was it an obscene call?"

He knew even as he asked it that he was wrong; an obscene caller might upset her, but it wouldn't cause the surge of fear that had reached him. Alex Logan was made of sterner stuff than that.

"Obscene?" She gave a harsh little laugh. "Parts of it, I guess. When he talks about . . . what he imagines I do out here, with seven men."

Michael reached for the gold tags that lay against his chest. Nothing. Either they didn't know, or he was on his own. He reached for her hands.

It hit him in a rush the instant he touched her, the horror of it, and his own anger rose up to meet it. It was all there, the crude suggestions, the lurid imaginings, whispered in an avid, almost eager voice. It was muffled, as if he were hearing it over the phone himself. ". . . all at once, or do you take them on one at a time, slut?"

Her hands were shaking beneath his, and he tightened his hold on her. And then the fear was there, the threat, and he knew why she was so frightened.

"It's more than that, isn't it?" he whispered. "He made some threats, didn't he?"

He felt a tremor ripple through her slender body, then felt her draw on an inner strength whose depth amazed him.

"I'm sorry, Michael. This isn't your problem."

"I'm making it mine. This isn't the first time, is it?"

She avoided his eyes.

"Alex?"

It was uncanny, Alex thought, the way she could feel his eyes on her. She lifted her head to look at him, because she seemed to have no choice.

"Trust me, Alex. I want to help."

She felt that warmth, that undeniable feeling of safety, of gentle protectiveness, once more. Trust him? Of course she trusted him. How could she not?

"Has it always been the same voice?"

She nodded slowly.

"But this call was different?"

"Yes." She shuddered, then steadied herself. "Before it was just...the filth. And saying I'd be sorry if I didn't close down the refuge." She laughed bitterly. "Of course, that's not what he called it. He has his own pet name for us. And for me. Especially for me." She shivered, her glance skipping to the phone again, then away. "It feels ... ugly. Vicious. So much hate..."

Michael curled his fingers around hers, sending her reassurance, using the full force of his mind to begin to build the shell of protection around her. When he felt her begin to respond, he spoke again.

"This call, it was different?" he prodded gently.

"This time..." She suppressed a shiver. "This time he said someone would get hurt."

He saw the tremor overtake her again and knew this was going to take more. He swung his feet up and pulled her into his arms. He leaned back against the four-poster's headboard and gently made her relax her tense body against him. She didn't fight him, a measure, he was sure, of her distress.

Something odd was happening, he thought. He wasn't supposed to feel the protection like this. It was supposed to be spun around her, a web of warm support. Yet he was feeling it, too, the succor, the warmth. A warmth that was threatening to become heat where she lay against him. His brows furrowed, puzzlement filling his eyes for a moment. This was truly peculiar, he thought, moving one hand to her chin to gently tilt back her head without really knowing why he did it.

Michael suddenly forgot that he wasn't supposed to get angry. He looked into Alex's wide, frightened green eyes and was tempted, very tempted, to plow a shortcut through this whole mess. Maybe he could get to whoever was behind this before the boss caught on.

Whoa, he thought suddenly. He stared at the top of her head as she at last let it rest on his shoulder. In all the time he'd been doing this, never once had he been tempted to violate the strict and often inexplicable rules that had been set down. Yet something about this woman . . .

"If you want to leave," she said with a little sigh, "I understand. I know you didn't count on this kind of trouble."

He realized she had misinterpreted his silence and the intensity of his gaze.

"An anonymous threat over the phone from some coward? You're not getting rid of me that easily."

"It's not . . . just that." She lifted her head. "We've had some other things happen. Little things, mostly. Fences knocked down, phone line cut, that kind of thing."

" 'Mostly?' "

She lowered her eyes. "We had a prowler one night, about three weeks ago."

Three weeks. About when Rick had shown up. Coincidence?

"Did you see him?"

"No. He . . ." She stopped, and he felt another ripple of emotion go through her. He tightened his arms around her and then he had it: anger. A good, healthy spurt of anger. Atta girl, he thought. After a moment, she went on.

"He went after Cricket. I heard him scream, that wild sound a stallion makes when he's ready to fight. I knew something had to be out there, but before I could get outside, I heard the fence go, and Cricket was out."

"You went outside alone?"

She looked puzzled. "He was trying to hurt my horse."

Of course she'd gone outside alone, idiot. What else would Alex Logan do when one of her own was threatened?

"Besides," she said, "I took Cougar with me. He ran him off. He would have had him, but he had a truck stashed up the road, and he got to it before Cougar could get to him. I would have gone after him, but I had to get Cricket before he got hurt." She grimaced. "I found the rocks he'd thrown at Cricket later."

"Where were the others? Why were you alone?"

"I wasn't. Sarah was here."

"Where?"

"In the house. She and Kenny have a room in the bunk-house, but she doesn't like to be alone when the guys leave."

"Leave?"

"Go up the hill." She saw his look and explained. "It's something Aaron came up with. A kind of therapy."

"Therapy?"

"When Aaron decided to stay here and help me, he went to school. He's a licensed therapist now. Anyway, they go up into the woods. They make a camp in some place they've never been to, then move on the next night and the next. It sort of simulates the situations they were in in Vietnam. Aaron says it makes it easier for them to talk."

"They leave you alone?"

"It's perfectly safe—"

She broke off at his look. "Okay, so it wasn't, that time. But he hasn't been back."

"Until tonight?" His eyes flicked to the phone.

"It may not even be the same person. Lord knows enough people don't want us here. Besides, I sort of thought that anyone who gets his thrills over the phone wouldn't have the nerve to show up in person."

"He sounds," Michael said dryly, "like exactly the kind of person who would chuck rocks at a horse."

Her eyes widened. "I . . . hadn't thought of that."

No, you wouldn't, Michael thought. You don't know anything about that kind of sick behavior. You're good and clean and honest, and so damn gutsy it makes me want to build a fortress around you to protect you from your own courage.

Hold it there, Justice, he thought. This isn't personal, remember? It never is. You're here to do a job, so get back to it.

"Did you tell anyone about it, when they got back?"

She lowered her eyes.

"That's what I thought. Have you told anyone about the calls?"

"I . . . they would only worry."

"Of course they would. They love you. But they should know, Alex."

"They have enough to think about, just trying to keep themselves together."

"So you carry the burden alone."

"Some of them spent years on the street before they came here, Michael. They had to deal with too much of this kind of thing out there. They came here for peace and a chance to heal. They need that chance."

He hugged her tightly, sending her as much serenity and security as he could. He'd never had to concentrate so hard before, but then, he'd never had this odd, inexplicable heat to deal with before, either.

"You're an amazing woman, Alex Logan. You're right, they need that chance. They deserve it. But think about something for me, will you? Think about the possibility that maybe, just maybe, they might need to be needed even more?''

She went very still. He could almost feel her thinking, feel her considering it.

"You can't protect them from the world, Alex. They're grown men, not children."

She gave a shuddering little sigh. "You're right. I have been, haven't I?"

"You were only trying to help."

"But I was treating them the same way I hate to be treated. Like a child." Her eyes flicked to the quiet telephone. "Although at the moment, that's what I feel like. Maybe they're right. Maybe I am just a silly little—"

"There's not a person here who would ever think of you as a 'silly little' anything," Michael said swiftly, positively. "Aaron has been here since the beginning, and Mark almost that long. You were only eighteen then, Alex. It's only natural that they still think of you that way. And the others take their lead from them, or else they knew of you before they ever got here, as Andrew's little sister."

"I suppose," she sighed.

It never occurred to her to wonder how he had become so well informed when these men were some of the most reticent in the world. They had accepted him now, she knew, and were probably much less wary of talking around him.

"And don't forget something else. Part of the reason they think of you as so young is that they feel so old themselves."

She looked at him. "I hadn't thought of it that way." She gave an embarrassed little laugh. "You'd think I'd be used to it by now. Kid sister to the world, that's me. Or kid brother. At least, it seems they think that, sometimes."

"No man with eyes is ever going to think that, Alex. You may wrap it like a boy, but the package is most definitely female. Very nicely female."

Alex flushed, wishing she could come up with some quick, witty remark. But if she tried, she admitted with rueful self-knowledge, she would say something utterly honest and utterly stupid. Like asking if *he* thought she was "nicely female." So for one of the few times in her life, she wisely decided to remain silent.

But she quickly found that remaining silent had its price. She became all too aware that they were on her bed, that her head was resting on his shoulder. His bare shoulder. He had on only his worn, soft jeans, and her hand was resting smack in the middle of his broad, muscled—naked—chest.

His skin, smooth and free of any hair to interfere with her sense of touch, felt like hot silk stretched taut over hard muscle. The heat of him seemed to infuse her, to make her feel oddly slack, so that she sagged against him. Involuntarily her fingers flexed, curling as the tips slid over that taut flesh.

She wondered what that sleek, smooth skin would feel like if she stroked it, if she let her hand slip down to his flat, hard stomach. She wondered what it would feel like to tangle her fingers in the scattering of hair that began at his navel. She wondered how his skin would feel beneath her lips if she leaned forward to kiss—

Oh, Lord, she thought, immensely grateful that he couldn't see her face. Although, she added in silent humiliation, he probably couldn't help but feel the heat from her flaming cheeks; she could only hope that he wouldn't guess the reason. She couldn't give him time to guess the reason, she thought hastily.

Her gaze fell on the rectangular tags that lay just above her fingertips. Thankful for the distraction, she moved to touch them, not surprised to find them warm from his body. Very warm. Well, not warm, exactly. And they didn't feel like the inflexible, hard metal she'd expected, either. In fact, she couldn't quite describe what they felt like.

"What are these?" she asked, lifting her head to look more closely, trying to ignore their enviable position in the center of his chest. She thought she felt him tense slightly, but he answered easily enough.

"A . . . family heirloom, sort of."

She lifted the golden tags, seeing that they were indeed the size and shape of dog tags. She tilted one to look at it, but it was hard to read the ornate script in the faint light.

"What does it say?"

"Just my name. And . . . birthday."

She shifted it closer to the light. Now that she knew, she could make out the sweeping swirls of letters and numbers. Numbers. She raised her eyes to his.

"Michael, this says September 29, 1850."

"There's been a Michael Justice around for a long time."

"And I suppose they've all been born on September twenty-ninth?"

"Of course." His tone was teasing, but there was something oddly serious in his eyes that made her wonder.

"Including you?" she asked.

He shrugged, his muscles flexing beneath her hand. "It's St. Michael's day. When else?"

"Oh. That's why you're Michael?"

"Sure. One day later and I would have been Sam."

She smiled. "But why dog tags?"

"Michael was the leader of the celestial armies, wasn't he?"

"Ouch." She gave a pained chuckle. "Someone has a warped sense of humor."

Michael laughed. *My sentiments exactly,* he thought.

"But they didn't have dog tags back then, did they?"

*Oops.* "I don't know. These were just . . . given to me."

"So this Michael Justice was the first one?"

"As far as I know."

"It must be nice, to know where you came from so far back. I don't know—what's this?"

She was holding up the second tag, angling it toward the light as she had the first.

"Why, it's a dragon," she said, answering her own question. She looked at him again. "Let me guess . . . Michael fought one, I suppose?"

"So the legend goes."

"Too bad there are none left," she said whimsically. "You're reduced to minor miracles."

She knew he had tensed this time. "What do you mean?"

"Just look at what you've done around here in only a week. I thought it would take a miracle to get everything done that needed doing, but I was wrong. It just took you."

She felt him relax. "You just need an extra pair of hands. And we're not done yet."

"It won't take long, at the rate you're going. It seems like you manage to do at least three things at once."

He shrugged again and gave her a teasing grin. "What can I do? Like you said, there aren't any dragons left to slay."

"If there were..." she began, but trailed off as she realized she'd been about to make one of her foolishly honest remarks.

"Alex?"

"I was just going to say," she said, her color high again, "that you were named appropriately."

He laughed. "Hardly. Michael was an archangel. I don't even work for the same guys. Couldn't. Angelic I'm not."

She took it as he'd meant her to, as a joke. "Just borrowed the name, huh?"

"Yep. Doesn't fit at all. Not like yours."

"Mine?" She looked startled.

"Yes. Didn't you know?"

"Know what?"

"Alexandra is the feminine form of Alexander, isn't it? It means 'defender of men.'"

"I didn't know." Nor, she thought, did she know how he'd found out her full name; she never used it.

"Now you do. And it fits."

She made a face. "Hardly. I'm not brave enough for that."

"You do an impossible job here, you're being terrorized by some crazy idiot and never say a word to anyone or ask for any help, and you don't think you're brave?"

She grimaced. "He was trying to scare me, and he succeeded admirably. I wouldn't call that particularly brave."

"But you kept going."

"I had to. Things had to be done. I couldn't let everybody down just because I was scared."

"Alex, Alex," he murmured, hugging her, "what do you think courage is?"

"It's not cowering over a couple of phone calls," she said sourly.

"No. It's being scared to death and saddling up anyway."

She blinked at him. "Did you just make that up?"

He grinned. "No. I think it was John Wayne." He was suddenly serious. "But he was right, Alex. Anyone who says he's never been scared is a liar, or a fool. And the ones who keep going in spite of it are the heroes."

Alex gave a shaky little sigh; what he'd said made sense, but she could hardly take the thought of herself as some kind of hero seriously.

"You make everything seem so...clear. You make me look at things in ways I never thought of before."

"That's what friends are for."

Friends. Was he? It certainly felt like it. Perhaps Aaron had been right; perhaps she was hungrier than she had realized for someone her own age.

"I didn't realize how much I needed a friend."

"You've been working too hard. For far too long."

"I had to," she said again. "For Andrew."

"Your brother?"

She nodded, the movement rubbing her cheek against his chest. Heat rippled out from beneath that small patch of skin touching skin. For a moment Michael found it hard to breathe. What was happening to him? Confused, he groped for what he'd been about to say. "Tell me about him," he urged her.

"I loved him," she said simply. "He was fourteen years older than me, but I think that made us closer. My earliest memories are of him playing with me, pulling me around in a wagon, and riding me in front of him on his horse.''

"Good memories."

"Yes. There are plenty of those. I try to concentrate on them instead of the others. I was six when he went to Vietnam, and I was crushed. He was my adored big brother who spoiled me rotten, and I missed him terribly. I must have driven my poor parents crazy."

"They waited a long time before having another child," Michael said, carefully not making it a question; she was opening up to him, and he didn't want to force it.

"They didn't think they could. My mother had Andrew when she was nineteen, and then she just couldn't get pregnant again. She was heartbroken. She'd wanted a houseful of kids. When she found out I was on the way, she was ecstatic."

Michael smiled. "There's no joy in the world like that of a child coming to those who want it so badly."

Alex stared at him, the beauty in his simple words catching her off guard. Sometimes, she thought, when those blue eyes are so alive and glowing, he seems so . . . so young and old at the same time, so wise and yet so innocent. . . .

She realized she was staring again and made herself go on. "Andrew went through a rough period when he found out. He'd been the only child for fourteen years, and then suddenly there was all this chaos about a baby he of course thought his mother was much too old to be having."

"But he took one look at you and fell for you like a ton of bricks."

Alex stared at him. "That's what my mother always said. How did you know?"

"Who wouldn't?"

She blushed, telling herself sternly that he was only teasing. "Anyway, I was devastated when he left. I used to live for his letters, although I don't think I quite understood how far away he was, or why he was there. But I'll never forget the day two years later when my parents got the telegram saying he was missing."

She shuddered at the memory. He held her tighter.

"We were so happy when he was found alive. We didn't care about anything else. Even when he came home in a wheelchair. He was alive. That was all that really mattered."

"But Andrew cared."

She sighed. "Yes. He hated being in that chair. He'd always been so active. He tried to hide it, especially from Mom and Dad, but—"

"But not from you."

"He had to have somebody to talk to, and I was there. Dad was working so hard here, and Mom had to go back to work in town, too, because the bills were so high and the government didn't pay for everything they wanted him to have. Andrew knew it was because of him, and he felt awful about it."

"How awful?" he asked softly, sending her another wave of reassurance.

"Very. I was only ten when he came home, but I remember gradually getting more and more scared for him. I was afraid to leave him alone, afraid he wouldn't be there when I came back. I didn't realize then, only later, looking back, that I must have sensed what he was thinking."

"About suicide?"

She nodded, glad this time for his perception. "Dr. Swan tried to get him to go for help, but he wouldn't. He just kept getting more and more depressed. He just sat for hours, in the room you're in...."

So that was what he'd sensed, Michael thought. He'd felt it that first night, the echoes of pain and surrender that seemed to have soaked into the walls.

"One day I found him with one of Dad's guns. He was just sitting there, looking at it, touching it, but it scared me so badly... I ran in and grabbed it from him. It was loaded, and it could have gone off, and I think that scared him, that I might have been hurt. He never did it again.''

Courage, he thought again. When it came to the ones she loved, Alex Logan would never come up short. She would have made a hell of a pioneer, he mused, thinking of the hardy men and women of that time. Then her voice jerked him out of his contemplation.

"Then, when I was about thirteen, he changed. He got the idea of a place, a place for guys who didn't get even the attention he got, because they weren't visibly hurt. A place to live away from the world that hated them—it was so much worse then—to be with others who understood, until they could survive back in the world."

"A dream can do a lot to keep a man going."

"It did," she said softly. "He started thinking of the future again, of what he wanted to do, where he would find the land, how to make it self-sufficient, so that when they dealt with the world it would be by choice, not necessity. He..." She swallowed tightly. "He always talked about how horrible it was to have the power of choice taken away. Theirs had been taken away when they were drafted and never given back."

"What happened?"

He knew, had known since that first day, but her need for the release of talk was strong, and he wouldn't deny her.

"He was doing so well, planning, designing—it's because of all his work that we've survived at all. But then...our parents were killed in an accident. It took the heart right out of Andrew. Oh, he held on for a couple of years, for my sake, I think. He didn't want to leave me alone. But he got gradually worse. Finally Dr. Swan had to put him in the hospital. It...didn't take long after that."

There was so much more to it than those simple words, Michael knew. He knew about the horror of a fifteen-year-old child having to identify the bodies of her parents because there was no wheelchair ramp at the small morgue. He knew about her struggle to hold on to the farm that had been her home, trying to work a job to supplement the small insurance policy, finish school, run the farm, and take care of Andrew all at the same time. He knew about a seven-teen-year-old girl growing up long before her time as she watched her beloved brother deteriorate before her eyes, crying out to her to help him end the pain.

"So you built his dream for him," Michael whispered as he held her close, feeling her exhaustion, willing her to rest. "You built it, and you made it work. He would be so proud of you, Alex."

"I hope so," she murmured. "He wanted it so much, once." She didn't understand why her eyes were suddenly so heavy; she only knew that the warm lassitude that was stealing over her was delicious, and very welcome.

"He would be," Michael repeated quietly. "Just like all of us. You've done so much for everyone you've helped here."

He changed the pitch and cadence of his voice to lull, to soothe, feeling her beginning to slip gently into sleep as he went on.

"So you've earned a rest, darlin'. You've done the job, and it's past time for you to stop and realize you're a woman now, and a beautiful one at that. No more thinking you're just a scrawny little tomboy, Lex."

Yes, Andrew.

Alex thought it hazily as the warm, pleasant fog closed in around her. He seemed so close, his dear voice so real as he talked to her just as he always had, the drawl he always put on for her as thick as ever. She wanted to ask, but she was so sleepy she could only think the words: Are you truly proud, Andrew?

The answer came back, clear and strong and certain, in the voice she loved and remembered so well. "Very proud, Lexie-girl."

The old, familiar nickname, used by no one but her be-loved brother, echoed sweetly in her ears. And with a little sigh of contentment she slid into a deep, dreamless sleep.

Michael held her for a long time, listening to her quiet breathing as he studied her finely drawn features: the pert nose with its faint scattering of freckles; the delicate line of her jaw; the twin sweeps of her thick, lowered lashes. He saw weariness in the slight shadow beneath those lashes and determination in the set tilt of her little chin. She tugged at him in a way he'd never known before.

He held her until he realized, with a little jolt of shock, that he was doing it more for himself than for her. And that he was shockingly aware of the fullness of her breasts pressed against him through the thin cloth of the long, worn T-shirt she slept in. And that the heat that had been merely puzzling before was rapidly becoming uncomfortable, making him want to do something to ease it. Making him want to touch, to caress...

Stunned, he carefully slipped out of the bed, tucking the covers around her. His mind was racing. What the hell was this? This wasn't supposed to happen. It never did, never had. Instinctively his hand went to the tags. Nothing. What was going on? Had they gone to sleep on him?

And then, just as he was about to send out a bellow that would rattle all their cages—or whatever they lived in—he stopped. He wasn't sure what he wanted to ask, or even *if* he did. And he was even less certain that he wanted an answer. He let the tags fall back on his chest. He stood there for a long time, looking at the slender form curled up in the big bed.

Only the creak of the back door being nudged open and the distinctive sound of Cougar's toenails clicking along the floor as he came back from his nightly rounds brought him out of it. And only when he moved his hand to tickle the big dog's ears did he realize that that hand had been pressed against the spot on his chest where her hand had rested.

"Watch her," he whispered to Cougar, then whirled and strode hastily out of the room. And while he had sent Alex into the peaceful slumber she so desperately needed, he was unable to help himself and lay awake long into the night.

# Four

———

"**I** can't go, either," Kenny said casually, running a hand through his thinning blond hair. "I have to get to work if we're going to get a third cutting out of that alfalfa."

"I don't need—"

"And I've got a huge stack of mending to do," Sarah said blithely. "So I can't go."

"If you'd just—"

"I have to see to that cut of Daisy's," Wheezer put in.

"I—"

"And I'm going to finish the barn door, now that Mike showed me how," Matt said swiftly.

"Guess it's up to you, Mike," Aaron said cheerfully.

"I keep telling you that I don't need—"

Steve cut Alex off easily. "You'll pick up Wheezer's medicine, won't you?"

"Of course. And I'm quite capable of carrying a bottle of pills without help, thank you."

"Remember, you promised never to go into town without at least taking Cougar with you," Steve reminded her. "And he's off with Mark somewhere." He turned innocently to Michael. "You don't mind, do you, Mike?"

Michael knew what they were up to, and it made him smile inwardly. It also made him nervous, but he wasn't quite ready to admit that yet, even to himself.

"Mind standing in for Cougar? Of course not."

Alex blushed. "You don't have to, really. I'll be fine. I'm just going into Riverglen, not Beirut."

"Doesn't seem much different, sometimes," Matt grumbled.

"I don't mind," Michael assured her. "In fact, I'd like to go. I haven't been into town yet."

Alex surrendered then, but grudgingly. She had a feeling they were all up to something, with her and Michael as the pawns in their little game.

"I'm sorry," she said as she steered the truck through the gate. "This really isn't necessary, but they just—"

"Worry about you. Like you do about them."

She sighed. "I know. But it's more than that. I think they maneuvered this whole thing."

"I know."

She glanced at him, startled. "You do?"

"It was a little...obvious."

"Oh." Her cheeks flamed.

"Don't be embarrassed, Alex. They care about you, and they feel guilty that you don't spend any time with people your own age."

"Like you?" She was watching the empty road as if it were a busy interstate.

"That seems to be what they've decided," he said carefully.

"I'm sorry."

"Don't be. I'm flattered."

She stared at him then. "Why? You could have anybody!"

His mouth twisted wryly. "Not exactly," he muttered under his breath before he answered her. "You're very precious to them, Alex. I'm flattered that they would trust me with you."

"Oh."

Her eyes went back to the road, and he could feel her withdrawal. He'd hurt her, he thought. Involuntarily his hand came up to reach for her, but a sudden memory of that growing, surging heat he'd felt while holding her stopped him. I'm sorry, Alex, he told her silently. I wish... Hell, I don't know what I wish anymore.

"The truck is really running well," she said in a rush, anxious to fill the gap. "Thank you."

"You're welcome. On a full tank, you should be able to make it to Portland and back without stopping for gas."

That earned him another look. "That's almost three hundred and fifty miles."

"Yes."

"Michael, this truck never went three hundred and fifty miles on a tank of gas in its life."

He shrugged. "I made some adjustments. I think it'll do it now."

She looked doubtful, but Michael noticed that she didn't quibble about whether or not she was going. He smiled inwardly; she was going to enjoy herself more than she realized. He turned to look out at the lovely, green Oregon countryside.

Their time in the little town was neither as bad as he'd feared nor as good as he'd hoped. He saw the looks she got, the cool greetings from those who didn't avoid her altogether, and there were a few nasty grumblings as they passed, but most of the people seemed merely wary, watchful rather than antagonistic, unfriendly rather than malevolent. And the majority of raised eyebrows seemed directed at him rather than her, and he could almost feel them assessing him, trying to figure out how he fit into the image they had of her and what she was doing at the refuge.

They weren't sure, he realized. His hopes rose; as long as their minds weren't set, they could be changed. He began to turn over possibilities in his mind as they walked down the small street.

Alex stopped at the little post office, taking the stack of mail the woman behind the counter handed her with a smile. "Thanks, Lucy."

"You're welcome, dear. How are you?"

Here, at least, was a friendly face, Michael thought, studying the pleasant looking, plump woman in the flowered dress.

"Fine, thanks." Alex introduced Michael, explaining that he would be there for a while.

"Welcome, Michael. I'm Lucy Morgan, town clerk, notary, postmistress, and general gofer." She eyed him curiously, but with none of the speculation or avidness others had. "Will you be expecting any mail?"

"No."

Somehow the single syllable sounded very forlorn, and Michael shifted uncomfortably. He hadn't meant it to sound that way and certainly couldn't be feeling that way. He'd always been alone; he was used to it, and it didn't bother him. Did it?

"—so sorry about what Frank said to you the other day."

The distress in the woman's tone brought Michael out of his musings.

"It's not your fault," Alex said with a little sigh. "I know he doesn't like the idea of the refuge."

"He just believes all those horrible things you hear, you know, about that traumatic stress thing, and people like that going on crazy shooting sprees."

"I know, Lucy. And I can't say it doesn't happen."

"But I remember your brother, Alex, and that sweet Gary Swan, God rest them both. If things had been different, it could have been them out there with you. They would never hurt a soul."

"No, they wouldn't. And neither would the men who are there now. They're just trying to get over a horrible experience they were never allowed to deal with before."

"That's what I try to tell Frank, but you know my husband. He's so stubborn."

"Keep trying, Lucy. He might come around."

"I will. But please believe me, he isn't behind that trouble you're having with the council. He may not like what you're doing, but he wouldn't interfere."

"I know." Alex gathered up the mail. "We have to stop by Dr. Swan's, so we'd better go. Thanks, Lucy."

"What," Michael asked when they were outside and heading for the small grocery store, "did her husband say to you?"

Alex shrugged. "Just the usual. He admits they need a place to go, but he doesn't want it in his backyard."

"That's all?"

Alex looked up at him. "He's not the caller, if that's what you mean. He's stubborn and set in his ways, but there's not a vicious bone in Frank Morgan's body."

Michael shrugged. "Just checking. What did she mean about the town council?"

"Somebody complained, said we should be closed down because we're in an area that's not zoned for what we do."

"What you do is unique. How could there be a zone for it?"

"Exactly." She sighed. "We're going to fight it at the town meeting this month, but I don't know what's going to happen. Mayor Barnum isn't overly fond of us, either."

"Don't worry," he reassured her, his mind racing as he wondered who was behind this attack, and whether it was the same person who was making the calls. "It'll be all right, Lex."

She stopped dead, staring at him. "Why did you call me that?"

Oops, Michael thought. You're getting sloppy here. Or you're just thinking too much about her and not enough about what you're doing. "I...heard one of the guys say it. But if you don't like it, I won't—"

"No, I...it's just that Andrew used to call me that."

"Oh. Sorry. I didn't realize it was...reserved."

"No," she said again, shyly, her cheeks flaming. "I don't mind if you use it."

Had there been an emphasis on that "you?" Maybe, he thought. Even if there was, that's no reason for you to go all mushy inside, he lectured himself. Lord, he was having a hard time with this job. He couldn't seem to pay attention to anything when she turned those green eyes on him. He tightened his jaw, determined to get back in the old, familiar, safe groove. Disquiet flickered through him as he wondered why he'd used the word "safe," but he smothered it as they reached their destination.

He held the door of the small grocery open for her, then wandered around as she gathered her purchases. He thought the woman at the checkout counter watched them a bit too closely, but he was more concerned about a group of boys, no more than thirteen or fourteen years old, who were clustered in one corner.

They eyed Alex avidly and began to have a lively, heated discussion among themselves. Michael saw her react as some of their whispered phrases reached her, saw her cheeks pinken as she handed the thin, middle-aged woman her money.

The woman took it as if it were tainted, handling it with two fingers as she stuffed it into the register. Here, then, was the enmity he'd been warned about. But, he thought, as long as it was only there in a few, it could be overcome. He would see to that. He stopped by the door to wait for her.

One of the boys, backed by his supporters, turned to look at Alex, and when he spoke it was obviously meant for her to hear.

"Hey, look guys, there she is. I'd like some of that, wouldn't you?"

As Alex's color deepened, Michael's head snapped around and he looked at the sniggering group. They didn't look at him, apparently not realizing he was with her.

"Yeah," the same loud voice came again. "My old man says she puts out for all of them out there."

Michael went rigid, then started toward them. Alex hastily gathered up her small bag and ran over to him.

"No, Michael." He turned to look at her, and she saw the fury in his eyes. "He probably doesn't even understand what he's saying. They're just kids."

"So was Jack the Ripper, once," he growled.

"It's not their fault. He's just...repeating what he heard from his parents."

For the briefest of moments her eyes flicked to the woman behind the counter. Michael didn't miss the movement and turned his head to look steadily at the woman. He saw it then, the resemblance in the sulky set of the mouth and the obdurate glint in the dark eyes. The woman glared back at first, her mouth twisted into a smirk as she crossed her arms over her stomach. Then, as Michael's gaze never wavered, she began to look uncertain, then shifted uneasily.

"Please, Michael, I don't want any trouble. It will only make things worse."

The loud-mouthed boy had fallen silent the moment he had realized he wasn't dealing with a lone female. He backed up a step, stopping only when he came up against a large stack of soup cans.

Alex held her breath as she watched Michael. There was something so elementally physical about him as he stood there, every muscle taut, his gaze now locked on the boy who was looking more nervous every second. He looked like what he was at that moment, an angry man ready for a fight and more than capable of winning it. Then she saw him let out a long, compressed breath, and the tension in him eased.

Only the pleading look in Alex's eyes and the youth of the boy stopped him. It had been a long time since he had resorted to physical violence, but he wanted to now. He wanted to pick up that kid by the heels and rattle him. He'd never felt such fury. The fierceness of the need to avenge the insult to her startled him, and he knew he'd better get out before it won.

As he held the door open for Alex, he saw the woman, smirk restored, reach out to close the drawer of her cash register. The boy was slower to react, relief still uppermost in his face as he watched Michael start out the door.

He almost made it. Another two seconds and he would have. But the boy opened his mouth just a fraction of a second too soon, and Michael heard him.

"Guess I told her what we think of her kind!"

Michael waited just long enough so that Alex wouldn't see before he looked back over his shoulder. She never heard the boy's startled yelp as the soup cans tumbled down on him, or the woman's squeal as the cash register drawer slid shut on two of her fingers. And by the time they reached the truck, Michael had his grin under control.

Alex didn't speak until she had pulled the truck into the parking lot of the small twelve-bed clinic on the edge of town. She shut off the engine, then turned to look at him.

"Thank you." There was only the slightest of quivers in her voice.

"For what? Not ripping the little moron's head off?"

"No. For wanting to."

He looked startled; then he laughed, that same full, joyous sound she had reveled in before.

"You're welcome," he said with a grin. "But that doesn't mean I won't do it later if he doesn't grow some brains."

Alex smiled tentatively, somehow not completely certain he was joking. She glanced at the door to the clinic, then back to him.

"Will you come in and meet Dr. Swan?"

"Yes. I'd like to."

She nodded, pleased, but her expression was troubled. "Would you . . . not mention what happened?"

"Why?"

She sighed. "He tries so hard to change the way people think about us. It would upset him to know it isn't working."

"With a couple of people, anyway," he muttered.

"I don't want him to worry about it. He's already done so much for us. He takes care of us when things get beyond Steve. He did all those tests on Wheezer and gave us the medicine for next to nothing. And he was always there for Andrew and me."

"Okay. Not a word."

He reached for the door but stopped when Alex didn't move.

"What's wrong?"

"I . . ." She glanced at him, then away. "It isn't true."

He looked at her blankly. "What isn't?"

"What Billy said."

"Billy?"

"In the store."

He drew back sharply. Anger flooded him, an anger that was tinged, amazingly, with hurt. He didn't stop to think that he wasn't supposed to be feeling things like that; he just reacted.

"I ought to rip *your* head off," he said gruffly. "Do you think I don't know that?"

"I didn't . . . I just wanted . . ."

He reached out to take her hands.

"Shh. It's all right. I understand. But don't be silly anymore. I know who you are, Alex Logan, and what you are. And no idiot kid spouting vicious garbage can change that."

Alex stared at him, then down at his hands covering hers. That sensation of calm, that feeling of peace and security, seeped into her again. She should have known, she thought. She should have trusted him to know. Why did she always feel this way when he touched her, so warm and safe?

And then something changed, shifted. The feel of his hands on hers became something else, something hot and exciting, and she felt her heart begin to race. She looked at his fingers around hers, tan and strong, and a sudden image of them touching her in other places flashed through her mind, making her take a quick, gasping breath.

He jerked his hands away, and she had the craziest feeling that somehow he had known what she was thinking. Color flooded her face, and she whirled around to jump hastily out of the truck.

Michael sat for a moment, shaken. The images had been so real, so vivid. His hands stroking her intimately, caressing her skin, cupping her breasts...

He sucked in a harsh breath. God, they were too vivid to have come from her, weren't they? Had they been his thoughts? Had he transmitted them to her somehow, in some strange glitch that went along with the other crazy feelings he'd been having? And why couldn't he tell where the thoughts had come from? He'd always been able to tell before. Before Alex, he'd never been confused like this.

And you'd damn well better stop it now, he ordered himself fiercely. Pay attention to the job. He slid out of the truck to follow her, forcing his rebellious mind to obey, to stick to the problem at hand.

He wondered if Billy or his malicious mother was behind the attacks on the refuge. Or the father. It seemed possible, especially if the boy had inherited his father's dirty mind and mouth.

Someone was just exiting the inner office as they came in, a young woman who greeted Alex civilly enough and turned a look of interest on Michael. Alex introduced them, refusing to acknowledge the pang she felt when the petite blonde eyed him with a look of pure feminine assessment.

"This is Marcy Thomas," Alex said. "She and I went to school together."

"Well, not exactly *together,*" Marcy simpered. "Alex is so much younger than I am." The disdainful look she gave Alex's slightly shaggy hair and plain jeans left no doubt that she meant too young, at least for a man like Michael.

She made it sound like a disease, Alex thought, and it was only two years anyway.

"Where are you from?" Marcy was asking, looking up at Michael from her five-foot height and managing to look helpless and fragile despite the fact that she could, Alex knew, swear like a Hell's Angel and drink several of the men in town under the table. Alex said nothing.

"I know you can't be from around here," Marcy trilled. "I know all the men here, and none of them could hold a candle to you!"

Subtlety, Alex thought wryly, had never been Marcy's strong suit. But the part about all the men she knew was probably true; Marcy had the fastest reputation in town. At least she had until they decided that Alex herself was a more interesting topic, she added bitterly.

Oh, stop being a bitch, she snapped at herself, feeling a rush of sympathy for the girl who had been the center of the town's gossip for so long.

"I came here from Denver," Michael was saying blandly, seemingly unmoved by Marcy's fluttering eyelashes and the way she reached out to touch him. "And before that St. Louis. I get around a lot."

"Oh, that's what I'd like to do, travel, see the world! I'm so tired of this boring little town!"

"I'm sure you are," he said smoothly. "It was nice meeting you, Ms. Thomas. But if you'll excuse me, I have to see the doctor now. Penicillin shot, you know."

He winked broadly at Marcy as Alex smothered a gasp. Marcy stared, wide-eyed, then stammered a hasty goodbye and scampered out the door.

"Michael Justice, you are terrible!" Alex exclaimed. "You know what she thought!"

"Yeah." He grinned crookedly. "I thought she might. Experience, maybe?"

"Michael!"

Alex tried her best to look aghast, but she couldn't quite stop a giggle. She was amazed that she was able to laugh at all. It was because of Michael, she thought. And this time she felt the warmth just by looking at his glowing blue eyes.

"Well, that's a pleasant sound I haven't heard enough of. I thought you'd forgotten how to laugh, young lady."

Alex smiled at the tall, lean, gray-haired man who had stepped out of his office.

"Hi, Doc," she said as she went to give him a swift hug. "This is Michael Justice. He's been our lifesaver this last couple of weeks. He's saved our time, our money, and our spirits more than once. Michael, Dr. Hank Swan, friend to this town, the refuge, and me."

"Doctor." Michael spoke with the quiet respect he used to the men of the refuge. It was sincere, and Dr. Swan sensed it immediately as he took the proffered hand.

"Call me Hank," he urged. "Or Doc, as Alex does."

"Okay, Doc."

"You're helping out at the refuge? Good," he said at Michael's nod. "It's certainly needed." He smiled fondly at Alex. "She can't do it all, no matter how stubborn she is about not admitting it."

"She's done wonders," Michael said.

"Yes, she has. But she needs to lighten the load, get some rest, like she's been promising me for years."

"I will, Doc," Alex said, and before she realized it, she was bubbling over with the news of her trip to Portland.

"Well, well, you *are* a miracle worker." Dr. Swan raised an eyebrow at Michael. "I've been after her since she was fifteen to take some time for herself."

But she wouldn't leave Andrew, and then she wouldn't leave the men at the refuge. Michael heard it as clearly as if the man had said it.

"I just wish it could be longer," he said softly.

"Oh, no," Alex said with an embarrassed laugh. "I feel guilty enough already."

"For taking two days off in eight years?" Michael asked dryly.

"But I—"

"Lex, if they can't last two days without you, you haven't done a very good job there."

Once again he stopped her dead with an argument she couldn't answer. She heard Dr. Swan's approving chuckle and turned to look at him wryly.

"Easy for you to laugh," she grumbled. "He does this to me all the time."

The doctor's clear gray eyes met Michael's for a moment. Then, without being sure why, Swan was nodding. "Good," he said succinctly. "It's about time someone slowed you down. Now," he went on briskly, "I assume you're here for Cyril's medicine?"

She nodded.

"Fine. I'll get it. You can wait in my office. I'll only be a minute."

"Cyril?" Michael whispered as he followed her through the waiting room door. "Wheezer's name is Cyril?"

Alex giggled. "Yep. Now you know why he doesn't complain about being called Wheezer."

"I guess so. I—"

He broke off, stopping dead as they stepped into a short hallway. He glanced around but saw nothing except a tall, thin man, escorted by a nurse, leaving one of the examination rooms. Nothing that explained the sudden prickling at the back of his neck, or the chill that had rippled down his spine.

"Michael? Are you all right?"

"Fine." He answered her automatically as they went into the office, trying to shrug off the eerie feeling; it was weaker in here, but it wouldn't go. Michael began to walk around the room, searching for any clue to the source of the icy sensation. He knew it had nothing to do with the doctor; nothing lay hidden behind those kind, gray eyes.

He came to a stop before a photo on the wall. It was of a young man in military uniform, and even with the difference in age, there was no doubt as to his parentage; the resemblance to Hank Swan was unmistakable. And it wasn't just in looks; after a moment of staring at the photograph, Michael knew two things. One, that the young man in the picture was his father's son in spirit and kindliness as well as appearance, and two, the sad realization that this gentle man had been taken from the world in a cold, ugly way.

Yet his spirit was here in this house, nearly strong enough even now to overcome the odd sense of malignancy he'd felt. Michael knew it was a measure of the love his father still felt for him, keeping him alive in heart and memory. No, the hostile presence in this place did not emanate from here, either, Michael thought.

"He was killed six months after he got shipped out. Near Da Nang. Doc was devastated. Gary was very special, to all of us." She looked at the picture, a sad fondness in her eyes. "He and Andrew were close, and I used to follow them around like a puppy. But Gary never minded. He used to carry me when Andrew got tired, and tell everybody that he was going to wait for me to grow up so he could marry me."

Michael opened his mouth to speak but found he couldn't get any words past the sudden tightness in his throat. Her poignant nostalgia moved him, but what truly bothered him was the odd feeling that settled in the pit of his stomach at what she had said about Gary marrying her when she grew up.

It should have seemed ridiculous, but Michael's mind wouldn't let go of it. It was ridiculous from a twenty-year-old to a six-year-old, but if he'd lived, would it have been so ridiculous from a thirty-four-year-old to a twenty-year-old Alex? Would she even now be settled in with him, with a couple of sassy, bright-eyed children? And why the hell wouldn't this knot in his stomach go away?

"Here we are."

They both turned to face the doctor as he came into the room. His eyes went briefly to the picture they stood in front of, and Michael felt the wave of love and lingering pain and longing that welled out from the man. But he said nothing except, "You tell Cyril I need to see him sometime soon, to make sure this dosage is still appropriate."

"I will, Doc. Thanks." Alex took the bottle.

The outer door was closing as they came out, and Michael caught a glimpse of that same tall, sallow-faced figure in the instant that the feeling hit him again; he felt a crawling sensation that made him shiver. It lingered in the waiting room like the pungent odor of a skunk long after the creature had passed. Was it connected to that disappearing figure, or to the clinic itself? Or someone else who was there, unseen? He shivered again.

Michael was glad to be out of there, glad to be rid of that repellent crawling sensation. A few minutes later he heard Alex groan under her breath as she pulled into the gas station.

"What?"

"Mr. Rodney," she muttered, gesturing toward the big black car parked on the other side of the gas pumps.

Michael turned to look. "And who," he asked, studying the pale, thin man who had several sparse strands of gray hair combed carefully over his shiny pate, "is Mr. Rodney?"

"President of the bank."

He absorbed this. "He's the one you were talking to, wasn't he? The day I arrived?" She nodded. "He's been giving you problems?" He eyed the man with a new suspicion; was he the one? I'm going to need a minute with him, Michael mused, and glanced at the hood of the man's car.

Alex sighed. "Oh, he's not as bad as some of the others. He doesn't like the idea of the refuge, but I think it's more because it offends his sense of tradition. Just like having a woman responsible for a considerable loan at his bank offends his perception of a woman's place."

"Barefoot, pregnant and in the kitchen?"

"'Fraid so."

"His loss."

She looked at him curiously. "Oh?"

"Women are the real strength of the world. The backbone." He grinned. "That's why they have the babies. If you left it to the men, mankind would have died out eons ago. No man could stand it."

She grinned; she couldn't help it. Then, as a muttered exclamation came from the car next to them, they both turned to look.

"Blasted car! Start!"

Mr. Rodney's face was red as he turned the key again. He was rewarded with a few seconds of rough, coughing engine noise, and then silence as the motor shuddered and died. The young attendant stood by scratching his head. There was no sign of Pete Willis, the regular mechanic who ran the station. Alex sighed; if he couldn't get it started, she would be trapped into offering the man a ride. Reluctantly she slid out of the truck.

"Problem, Mr. Rodney?"

The pale man's paler eyes looked her up and down in dismissal. "That's quite obvious, isn't it, Miss Logan?"

Alex rolled her eyes as the man got out of the car, but she kept her voice level. "It sounds kind of like the truck did when I had a couple of spark plug wires loose."

"And just what would you know about it?" Rodney said condescendingly.

"Let her take a look, Mr. Rodney. You might be surprised."

Alex gaped at Michael as the skinny man eyed him suspiciously, obviously trying to remember if he knew him. Michael looked back blandly. The man was petty, tight-lipped, and rigid, but after a moment of intense concentration, Michael knew that he was too wrapped up in his own little world to be the one he was looking for.

"Go ahead, Alex."

Michael winked at her as he urged her forward with a gentle hand at her back. Bewildered, she went, aware as she leaned over the fender that Michael set up a stream of chatter with the equally bewildered Mr. Rodney. She stared at the engine compartment that was much more complicated than her relatively simple truck and wondered what on earth he expected her to do.

At last, for lack of anything else, she reached out and pushed down the spark plug wires, thinking that perhaps one truly was loose. They seemed secure, and she straightened up, looking at Michael in confusion.

"Go ahead and try it now," he urged Mr. Rodney, who wore the smugly disdainful look of a man about to prove a woman's foolishness as he got back into the driver's seat. He turned the key and got the same results; his expression grew even smugger. But before he could voice his complacent superiority, Michael gave the struggling engine a quick look, and it roared to life. Rodney was stunned into silence, gaping at the car as if it had just grown wings. And Alex was looking at it with even more surprise.

"Ah, women," Michael said melodramatically. "Just think what a wonderful world this will be when they run it."

"Never!" Mr. Rodney exclaimed automatically, finding his tongue at last.

"Don't count on it," Michael said, an odd glint in his eyes, as if he were looking at something only he could see.

The older man muttered something unintelligible, and reached to close the car door.

"We'd better be getting along," Michael said lightly. "You can just thank Alex, and then we'll be on our way."

"Michael!" Alex protested. "I didn't—"

"Nice work," he interrupted, reaching out and tugging on her arm to bring her around to face the flustered Mr. Rodney. Then he looked at the man pointedly.

"Er, thank you, Miss Logan." It sounded as if it had nearly choked him, and without another word he shut the door and drove off.

Alex stared after him, then shifted her nonplussed gaze back to Michael.

"I've heard men get teeth pulled with less pain," he said with a grin. "Without anesthetic."

"Michael, I didn't do anything to his car."

He shrugged. "You obviously did something. It sounded like what you said. Maybe it was just a loose wire." He grinned again. "With any luck at all, it'll die on him again. Preferably in the middle of nowhere."

She laughed, the look on Mr. Rodney's face when he had to thank her sweetly fresh in her mind. Her mood lasted as they drove back to the farm, and she even admitted she was looking forward to her trip to Portland.

"You just be careful, and remember you're there to relax."

"Yes, sir," she said meekly.

Michael looked at her sharply, then, when he saw the teasing glint in her eyes, burst out laughing. Alex smiled, thinking she would do a lot more than pretend docility to hear that laugh. It comforted her, in an odd sort of way, and not just because it convinced her that he couldn't really have read her earlier, steamy thoughts.

They—or rather Alex—talked easily, Alex marveling at how much she had suddenly found to say and Michael listening intently, encouraging her. They were nearly to the farm when he jerked his head around suddenly, staring ahead.

"What is it?"

He didn't answer right away; he just leaned toward the open window, tilting his head back. He looked, Alex thought, like some wild creature that had scented danger, and she felt an odd shiver go up her spine.

"Michael?"

"Something's wrong," he muttered.

He looked so forbidding that she didn't ask, just tried to control the fear he was instilling in her. He leaned farther out the window, nostrils flaring.

"Something's on fire," he said suddenly.

Alex smothered a little gasp. It had been an unusually dry year; a fire could be disastrous. She sniffed the air, but she could detect nothing. Yet he'd been so positive that she couldn't doubt him.

They went on a little farther, and then she, too, could smell it. Unconsciously she sped up. They made a wide turn, then crested a small rise, and Alex's heart leaped into her throat. Straight ahead, from the direction of her home, rose a black, ominous cloud of smoke.

# Five

The smoky pall grew thicker the closer they got to the farm. Tears began to well in her eyes, and she didn't know if they were from the smoke or the fear that was building in her.

"It's all right," Michael said suddenly.

She turned her head to look at him.

"It's not the refuge."

Her eyes widened, then flickered back to the road.

"How...?"

"It's not. Trust me, Alex."

She could feel it, that reassurance stealing over her. She knew that if she looked at him again his eyes would hold that radiance that lit them from within, that glow that made her feel so certain he was right. He would never let anything hurt her, she thought, then wondered where those words, so immediate and sure, had come from.

Yet she didn't question them; she just drove. As the road made another turn the air seemed to clear a little. Although she hadn't doubted him, she was relieved to pull into the long driveway at the farm and see that he was right. The gray, acrid cloud hung in the sky to the west, a safe distance away.

Matt, followed by Steve and Kenny, met them in front of the house.

"Do you know where it's at?" Alex's words tumbled out as she scrambled from the truck.

"No, Aaron drove over to look. He should be back—"

They all turned at the sound of a car and saw Aaron's battered little convertible pulling into the drive.

"It's about five miles over," he said as he dragged his lanky frame out of the low-slung car. "We should be fine."

"What is it?" Alex asked, eyeing the smoke nervously.

"Brush, for now. But it's closing in pretty fast."

"On what?"

Michael was looking at Aaron rather than the cloud or the others who had joined them to hear the report, including a capering Cougar, nudging Alex for attention.

"A couple of the places off the mill road." He pulled his glasses off and wiped them on his shirttail.

Alex's head came around swiftly. "The Morgans'?"

"That the little dairy farm?"

"Yes."

Aaron nodded. "The guy was arguing with the firemen. They want him to evacuate, in case they can't hold."

"But it's only him and his son," Alex said. "He'll never get his stock out."

"That's what they were arguing about. He says he won't go, not unless they help him get his cows out."

"And if they help him, they won't be able to stop the fire. There's not enough of them." Alex looked back at the rising gray haze.

"There could be."

They all looked at Michael. "What?" Matt said.

"If we helped."

"Us?" Kenny looked startled.

"Why?" Steve said, a little bitterly. "They'd be sitting back cheering if it was us."

"Exactly."

Aaron looked thoughtful, the others dubious.

"They think the worst. Give them the best instead." Michael concentrated on Aaron, knowing his best target. "Make them think."

Slowly, Aaron nodded. "Guilt can be a powerful thing." He looked around at the others. "You all know that."

"Guilt?" Sarah asked, puzzled.

"How would you feel if someone you'd judged without really giving them a chance did something good for you?"

"Guilty," she admitted.

"And," Aaron went on, "what would you do afterward?"

"I don't know. Wonder if I'd misjudged them, I suppose."

Aaron let her words stand as he glanced at Michael, who nodded in approval. Then he looked at the others.

"Well?"

"Do you really think it might work?" Kenny asked doubtfully.

"It can't hurt."

For a moment they wavered. Then Alex spoke. "I'm going to change into my jeans and boots." They all looked at her. "I've always wanted to know if Cricket had any cow horse in him. Cougar—" she bent to the big dog "—find Mark, boy. Go find Mark."

The dog let out a yelp and took off, Alex straightened up, and it was suddenly decided.

"I'll get our shovels," Matt said.

"I'll get my gear," Steve said. "Might need it."

"Alex, you got my pills?" She nodded and handed Wheezer the bottle from her pocket. "Good. Then I can help with the cows."

"Me, too," Aaron said quickly.

They scattered in all directions, even, after a moment of grudging hesitation, Rick. Alex turned toward the house but stopped when Michael reached out to touch her arm.

"I'll saddle Cricket for you," was all he said, but there was the warmth of a salute in his sky blue eyes.

"Thanks," she said, wondering why her voice sounded so funny.

When she came back out the others were gathered on the drive, loading shovels, blankets, and anything else they thought might be useful into the back of the truck. Sarah had filled several containers with water, and she put them in along with some plastic cups. Cricket was dancing, testing Michael's grip on the reins, sensing that something unusual was afoot.

"I'll take the back way," Alex said as she steadied the animal with a pat on the neck. "I should get there about the time you do."

Michael nodded and handed her the reins. They heard a ringing bark and looked around to see Cougar racing toward them, Mark hot on his heels.

"I'll explain to him," Michael said. "You take Cougar with you."

She nodded and swung up into the saddle with a smooth, graceful movement. Cricket snorted and gave a little crow hop, but Alex brought him down easily.

"Easy now, love," she crooned, stroking the black-and-white neck. The horse arched into her touch and whickered softly. An odd quiver went through Michael, followed by a blast of that persistent heat he couldn't understand or seem to avoid. He felt his muscles tense, ripple, as if they, too, wanted to feel the stroking caress of her hand. He clenched his jaw. He was going to have to have help with this, he thought. He didn't know what was going wrong, but he couldn't deal with it much longer.

Alex looked at him for a long moment, as if puzzled, then whirled the horse on his hindquarters and was gone.

\* \* \*

When the men arrived at the mill road, now blocked off by parked fire trucks, the beleaguered, sweat- and ash-covered young fireman there took one look at them and the equipment they'd brought and welcomed them openly.

"Boy, can we use you! We're holding the line but just barely. And that old coot won't budge without his damn cows."

"We'll help there, too, and more's on the way," Michael said. "You need a ride back up?"

The man nodded and joined the others in the back of the truck. He gratefully accepted the water Sarah poured for him, then looked around at them as he drank.

"You're from the Logan place, aren't you?"

Matt eyed the man warily. "Yeah. So?"

"Nothing." The man finished the water, then met Matt's gaze. "My dad died in the Tet offensive," he said simply.

After a moment Matt nodded in acknowledgment. "I was there. But I was luckier."

"Supposedly," the man said, and a look of understanding passed between them.

It was followed by an odd look of speculation on Matt's face, a look that Michael noted with interest. That's it, he thought. Think about it, Matt. There are more like him around. Just give them a chance.

When they arrived at the fire line, there was no time for any more talk. The flames were creeping closer, feeding voraciously on brush that was all too ready to burn after the uncommonly dry spell. The man in the white fire-captain's helmet who was directing the desperate efforts to hold back the tide of flame welcomed them without question.

"We've got four with shovels, one medic, and two to help with the animals, plus a rider on the way," Michael reported quickly. "And I'll fill in wherever you need me."

The man nodded gratefully and snapped out some quick directions. They scattered to do as ordered, and the battle began. It was hot, horrible work, and breathing the acrid, stinging air seared their lungs. They dug a firebreak, then had to drop back and dig another when the first was jumped by the racing flames. Steve was busy with several minor injuries, and Michael barely had time to look up now and then and check on Alex.

She made a dramatic picture as she rode the black-and-white horse through the milling black-and-white Holsteins. The animals were restless, agitated by the smoke and the crackle of the flames that were closing in. Several times they tried to break away, but she always seemed to be there to stop them.

Cricket the cow horse, he thought with a grin. And Cougar the cow dog, he added as the big animal raced after a bolting cow and herded her back to the main group that Alex was urging out onto the road.

She rode with a supple grace that fascinated Michael and a daring that made him afraid for her; one misstep by the dancing stallion and she could go down beneath the scrambling hooves of the cows. He had to force himself back to his own task of scouting the flank of the fire and marking the path for the firebreak they were trying desperately to get done before the flames reached the buildings.

He didn't know how long he'd been driving the flat-bladed shovel into the dirt when he looked up from his digging to see a gray-haired man in soot-stained overalls desperately spraying the sides of the barn with a small hose. The roof was already ablaze, sending embers up into the breeze. It was hopeless; the fire captain had ceded the barn in the effort to save the house, but the man refused to quit.

Michael was ahead of the others, changing the course of the firebreak to protect the house, when something made him look back at the barn once more. At first he saw nothing but the stocky figure of Frank Morgan, still fighting a lost battle. Then he heard an ominous crack, and as clearly as if it were outside instead of hidden in the flaming building, he saw the main beam give way.

Without a second's thought he dropped his shovel and launched himself toward the now-engulfed barn. He covered the twenty yards in less than two seconds.

Frank Morgan let out a startled shout as he was hit by a hundred and ninety-five pounds of solid muscle. They went down hard, Michael rolling until the man was beneath him.

"Hey! Stop, I—"

It seemed as if all the fires of hell were raining down on them as the beam gave way and the roof caved in. The air was thick with smoke and ash and flame. Michael felt a thud across his back and shoulders, felt the pressure, the heat, but no pain. He hunched over the man protectively, sensing rather than seeing the embers drifting down over them.

"Michael!"

He heard Alex's scream, a terrified, heartrending sound that made him shiver to the bone despite the fierce heat radiating around them. He could feel the thud of Cricket's hooves through the earth, then felt them come to a sudden halt.

"Michael! Oh, God, Michael!"

The sheer dread in her voice galvanized him. He braced his hands on the ground and lifted, feeling a heavy weight sliding away. He rolled to one side, off of Frank Morgan's overall-clad form. Then Alex was there, her arms going around him as he sat up.

"Michael," she said breathlessly. "God, I saw the roof go. I thought you were..."

She shuddered violently. His eyes met hers, and he read the lingering fear there, fear for him. Something knotted up inside him, tightening as he watched her eyes go over him, felt her hands touching him, as if she couldn't believe he had escaped unscathed.

"I'm fine," he managed to get out. Please, he thought dazedly, don't touch me. It feels too... too...

"You're really all right? That beam was right on top of you. I thought sure—"

"I'm fine," he repeated, more steadily this time.

Her hands had come up to cup his face, her eyes searching his. Her lips were parted for her quick, short breaths, and he felt a heat more intense than the fire begin to uncurl deep inside him.

He had to stop this, he thought a little dizzily. He lifted his hands to tug hers away, to stop that touch that felt so good. Instead he found himself pressing against them, holding her soft palms to his face.

"Michael," she breathed, her tongue coming out to wet lips dried by panic. He heard an odd, choked sound; it was a moment before he realized it was his own groan.

"What the... ?"

They pulled apart at the dazed sound of Frank Morgan's voice. As she recovered her composure, Alex's gaze went to the man as he gingerly sat upright, staring at the still-smoking crossbeam that lay next to him. His eyes went to the fallen roof of the barn, and his wonder that he wasn't dead showed plainly on his face.

"Are you all right, Mr. Morgan?" Alex asked quickly.

"Yes," he muttered, obviously still shaken. "Thanks to him." His eyes had shifted to Michael, then focused on Alex. "Alex?" His ash-smeared brow furrowed. "What are you doing here?"

"We came to help."

He stared, then looked around at the other men who were digging furiously and hosing down the roof of the house under the direction of the fire captain.

"Those men ... they're from your place?"

She nodded.

"Why?" he asked, stunned anew.

Her eyes went to Michael as she opened her mouth to give him the credit, but he forestalled her with his own simple words.

"We're neighbors." He scrambled to his feet and held out a hand to the still dazed man. "Better go to the first-aid station and get checked out."

Nodding somewhat numbly, he walked off. Alex turned her attention back to Michael, staring at the numerous holes that had been burnt into his shirt. There was a wide, black, charred stripe across his back, where the beam had fallen, but he appeared unhurt.

"Are you sure—"

"Alex, I'm fine," he said patiently. Then he went on, his carefully even expression denying the moment that had just happened between them. "You got the cows moved?"

He could almost feel the effort she made to shake off the lingering effects of those moments of terror. And of that frozen, electric instant in time. He could almost see her shoving away the turmoil, could almost hear her silent self-lecture.

"Yes, we did. They're all penned up down the road." She managed a smile. "You'd swear Cricket had been doing it all his life. And Cougar had a ball. Got to chase cows without getting in trouble."

He smiled back at her then, warmth returning to his eyes and banishing the last of her fright.

"I think they've got the upper hand now," he said, glancing over his shoulder. "Looks like the house is safe."

"Thank goodness. Lucy would have been devastated."

"I'm glad, then, for her sake." I'd be glad for anyone who was decent to you, he thought. "I saw her earlier, taking some things out of the house. Somebody must have called her."

"I want to go find her, see if there's anything she needs."

"If she saw her husband, she's probably at the first-aid station."

Alex nodded. She meant to go but couldn't quite relinquish the sight of him yet.

"Looks like you had a close call here."

They turned to look at the weary man in the white fire helmet.

"I wouldn't want to make a habit of it," Michael said wryly.

"I wanted to thank you. You people turned the tide for us. I don't doubt that we would have lost the house if you hadn't shown up."

Those words came back to Alex that night as they all sat around the table. They looked tired but quietly pleased with themselves. Even Rick wore a slight smile, although, as usual, he said nothing. They knew they'd done something good, she thought. They'd been needed, and they'd responded, thanks to Michael's nudging.

Michael. He'd been so right. They needed that feeling. They had needed to be needed. Not to be appreciated or thanked, just needed. Her eyes went to him, savoring the sight of him, remembering that heart-stopping moment when she'd been afraid he lay dead beneath that flaming, crushing beam. And the heart-starting instant when they had been locked in some frozen twist of time, touching with their eyes as much as their hands.

It was foolish to dwell on that moment, she told herself. And foolhardy to think it had been anything more than a fierce reaction to survival. Michael Justice had bigger and better things to do than waste his time with some naive country girl who was spellbound by him. The thought brought on a tightness in her chest that made it difficult to breathe. Involuntarily, she looked at him.

He was laughing at something Wheezer had said, his eyes alight and the dimple flashing. He'd become a part of them, a part of their lives so thoroughly now that it was hard to remember when he hadn't been here. And impossible for her to think of a time when he would be here no longer. She lowered her gaze to her plate, blinking rapidly.

"I heard the Morgans don't have enough insurance to rebuild the barn."

Alex looked up as Michael spoke; she knew that tone. It was the same one she heard just before he made her think of something she never had before, or think in a new way.

"That's rough," Aaron said.

"They have enough for the material but not the labor."

He left it at that, but the seeds he had planted today found nourishment in the good feelings they were enjoying, and Matt's grin was only slightly wry as he met Michael's eyes.

"And I suppose you figure we ought to volunteer?"

Michael shrugged. "Did I say that?"

"No," Kenny said dryly. "But you do have a less than subtle way of hinting."

"Me?"

Michael struggled to look innocent and failed utterly. Wheezer laughed and tossed a biscuit at him. Then they all laughed, and Alex had to blink against the brimming of her eyes again at how completely they had accepted him.

"Gonna build a barn?"

They all laughed at Mark's reduction of things to the essentials. Then Matt glanced around the table at everyone, one by one. The answer was obvious.

"I guess we are, buddy."


"—and then we'll start the . . . Alex, are you listening to any of this?"

Alex jerked her attention back to Sarah, her cheeks tinged with pink. She knew she'd been staring, but she couldn't seem to help it. She wished she weren't so helpless with a hammer, although she thought that maybe some pounded fingers would be worth the distraction.

"I can't blame you," Sarah said with a little laugh as she looked over to where the framework of the new barn now rose above the newly leveled and graded spot that had held the ashes of the old one. "Even though I'm crazy about Kenny, I wouldn't deny myself the pleasure of looking at that."

Alex's color went from pink to red. She busied herself with setting lunch out on the table, but it didn't matter. The image she'd looked so hastily away from was burned into her mind.

It was an unusually warm day, and as the work proceeded many of the men had pulled off their shirts. Including, to Alex's heart-pounding dismay, Michael. She had begun by staring in fascination at the flex and play of the muscles in his back and shoulders as he worked on one of the walls they would soon raise. Then, when the wall went up, so did her blood pressure, as Michael turned around to help lift the framework.

His worn jeans rode low on his narrow hips, emphasizing the broadness of his chest. She stared at the sweat-sheened smoothness of his skin, swallowing tightly when a bead of perspiration trickled down his chest, through the sparse trail of hair at his navel, then down below his waistband.

Only when Sarah's words had teased her out of her rapt entrancement did she realize that all he would have had to do was look at her and everything she was feeling would no doubt be written all over that silly face he found it so easy to read.

"Don't be embarrassed, girl," Sarah said kindly. "You need a little excitement in your life. And that," she glanced back at Michael, "is enough excitement for any woman."

Alex couldn't help the little sigh that escaped her. Sarah was kind, gentle, and loving, and had been her closest female friend for a long time despite the difference in their ages, but she had probably never suffered a moment of the kind of uncertainty Alex was feeling. She had loved Kenny since they were children, had married him when she was sixteen, and had stood by him through thick and thin, war and the shaky peace that followed.

"Now, what was that for? You can't tell me you haven't thought about it, child. I've seen you looking at him."

Alex carefully lined up the silverware. "And looking is as close as I'll get," she muttered.

"What do you mean?"

She sighed. "Look at him, Sarah. He could have any woman in the world with a snap of his fingers."

"What's wrong with that, as long as it's you?"

Alex flushed again. "Why on earth would it be?"

"Oh, so that's it, is it? Well, I've got news for you, dear. As much time as you spend sneaking peeks at him, he spends watching you when you're not looking."

Alex made a small sound of disbelief, but the descent of the men hungry for lunch stopped any further discussion. Alex kept her eyes carefully on her plate as she ate; Michael, still shirtless, was sitting next to her, and she didn't dare risk looking at him for fear of what silly thing she might say or do. But she did look up at last, when Frank Morgan stood up at the head of the long table they'd set out under the trees in the front yard.

"Er, I'd like to say something. My wife tells me I'm as stubborn as a Missouri mule, and maybe that's true. But when I know I'm wrong, I admit it." He coughed. "Well, I was wrong about you folks, and I'm sorry. And I'm downright glad you're my neighbors."

He sat down quickly, as if embarrassed. He didn't need to worry; all the eyes at the table were on Michael. He just smiled, not even the slightest touch of "I told you so" in his expression.

The barn was done by the time Saturday dawned. All of them gathered around as Alex was getting ready to leave for her weekend away, postponing their busy day long enough to say goodbye to her. They had beaten down all her protests about leaving them to catch up with all the work that had piled up while they'd been working on the barn, threatening to kick her out if she didn't go voluntarily.

"The reservations are all made, so get moving," Steve told her gruffly.

"Yeah," Matt said. "We don't want to see this ugly truck again until Sunday night."

"Fun, Alex," Mark said as he restrained a confused Cougar. "Have fun."

She sighed.

"Don't worry," Michael said. "This is for you. Don't worry. Don't even think about anything but yourself for a change."

He reached for the truck door at the same time she did, and their hands met on the handle. The moment she felt his touch, the anticipation she'd lost in the face of all the work she was leaving behind returned.

"Be careful," he said softly. She looked up at him, and for a long, silent moment their eyes locked.

"You gonna kiss her goodbye or what?"

Alex colored at Steve's remark, but Michael just smiled gently as he leaned forward to press his lips on her forehead. Alex's blush deepened again at the casual touch; a kid sister kiss, she thought, dispirited.

"Aw, come on, Mike! If you're gonna kiss her, kiss her!"

Alex could have cheerfully strangled Kenny at that moment. She lifted her head to say something, anything, to get out of this horribly awkward situation, but before she could speak, Michael moved.

She caught a fleeting glimpse of the battle in his eyes, but before she could decide what it meant, his mouth was on hers. Searing, piercing heat shot through her, melting away her embarrassment and her resistance. His lips were soft and gentle on hers, and she felt his hands come up to cup her face. His fingers threaded through her hair as he tilted her head back, and she heard an odd sound come from him at the same time that she felt his muscles tense, as if he were trying to back away and failing.

Then she was pulled hard against him, and his kiss became suddenly hot, fierce. Her head reeled as he ignited flames as blistering as those he'd fought, and she sagged against him.

"All right!"

"Whoooie!"

The assorted whistles and exclamations broke the spell, and Michael broke the kiss. Alex stared at him, her face flushed with a heat that had nothing to do with embarrassment. His own breath was coming quickly, and she could see the pulse beating rapidly in the hollow of his throat.

"Alex," he said thickly, shaking his head slowly.

She saw the pain in his troubled eyes and felt a sudden, frantic need to escape before he could say something that would shatter the sweetness of that kiss. She wanted to cling to it, savor it. She would face reality when she came back, but for now she wanted to hug this memory to her with the desperation of someone who thought it was the only thing she would ever have. She followed that instinctive urge and scrambled into the cab of the truck.

Michael stared after her as she drove away, heavy swallows alternating with his harsh breathing. He felt them all looking at him and started to move. He nearly staggered but kept going; he had to get away, had to calm down, had to think. His steps quickened; then he broke into a run. He didn't stop until he was into the trees behind the house, safe from curious eyes. He found a small, grassy clearing and sank to his knees. He knew he was shaking, but he couldn't seem to stop.

*Michael?*

A throttled sound of protest broke from him. Not now. I can't handle this now.

*Michael, are you there?*

They weren't going to go away. He knew that, because the signal wasn't usually this strong without direct contact. He grabbed the golden tags.

Go away.

*Ah, you are there. We got the oddest signal a few minutes ago. A burst of static.*

They'd felt it. They just hadn't figured it out yet. He barely managed to drop the tags before the memory blazed through his mind. The feel of Alex's soft lips, the unexpected jolt of pure, sizzling pleasure that had rocketed through him as she went warm and pliant in his hands.

*Michael? Are you still there?*

He took a deep breath and grabbed the tags again. And sent the message again.

Go away.

*Go away? Really, Michael, we haven't heard from you—*

I've been busy.

*Well, of course you have. But there are such things as regular reports, remember?*

Right. Sorry.

*Something wrong, Michael? You sound... odd.*

He dropped the tags again. He had to get a grip, he told himself severely. He didn't understand what the hell was happening, and until he did, he wasn't about to let anybody know about it.

*Michael? There is something wrong, isn't there? Do you need some extra help?*

He laughed harshly. I need help period.

*We keep losing you, Michael. Are you having transmission problems?*

Steadying himself, he grasped the tags again.

No.

*That's much better.* A pause. *We don't mean to bother you, Michael, but we were concerned. You're usually so punctual about checking in. What have you been doing?*

Fighting fires. Building barns.

Puzzlement came through. *Commendable, certainly, but—*

Never mind. I'll give you a report.

*All right. Ready when you are.*

He tightened his grip on the tags and sent it to them. Carefully edited. He'd never done that before; he could only hope it worked. It seemed to, for he got a calm answer when he was done.

*Congratulations, Michael. You've accomplished more than we expected so soon. When do you think you'll be done?*

Pain, sharp, biting, and instantaneous, grabbed him.

*Heavens, what was that? Are you all right?*

No, damn it, I'm not.

For once they ignored the curse. *What is it? Something's very wrong, isn't it?*

Forget it.

*But, Michael—*

Forget it. Please.

*Please? From you?*

I'll keep on top of the reports from now on.

*Michael—*

Later.

He let the tags fall back to his chest, then let out a tremendous, shuddering sigh. He should have told them, he thought. He should have asked what the hell was happening to him. He'd quit counting the years that he'd been doing this, but never in all that time had he felt anything like this. Maybe something was wrong with him. Maybe he needed a recharge or something.

Or maybe he was just plain worn out. Did people like him retire? It had never come up, and he'd never asked. But he supposed it couldn't go on forever. Nothing did. But he'd never thought about it until now. Just like he'd never thought about the fact that he never stayed when the job was done. Or that when he moved on he was alone. Always alone. It never bothered him. It wasn't supposed to bother him. They'd promised him that. They'd promised him . . .

He sat in the shadowed little clearing for a long time, the image of Alex in his mind and the feel of her on his lips.

# Six

Michael's head shot up, and he nearly dropped the crossbar he'd been nailing on the new barn door when he heard the sound of a car in the drive. Alex? Had she changed her mind? Come back?

He was out the door and halfway around the building when he skidded to a halt. Of course she hadn't. He would have known. He started to walk again, slower this time, but came to a halt again as he rounded the corner of the barn.

A police car? He blinked, but it didn't go away. And neither did the man in uniform standing beside it, talking to Matt. Michael eyed him curiously as he slowly walked the rest of the way.

The man was about thirty, tall and spare, with medium brown hair showing under his hat. A rather scraggly moustache shadowed his upper lip. He was pleasant looking enough, with light brown eyes that seemed oddly ingenuous, considering his profession.

Matt introduced him as Deputy Walt Howard. There was wariness in Matt's demeanor but no outright dislike, and when Michael shook the deputy's hand, he knew that the artless openheartedness was genuine.

"Anyway, like I was saying," Matt went on, "she took a trip up to Portland."

"Alex? But she never goes anywhere."

"Well, she did this time." Matt's eyes flicked to Michael, noticing how his casual scrutiny of the deputy had suddenly become more intense. "I'll tell her you stopped by."

"Do that, thanks. But actually, there's something else I needed to talk to her about."

"Anything I can help you with?"

Walt considered for a moment. "Maybe. Been a few livestock killings, last week or so. Looks like an animal brought 'em down."

"Sorry to hear that, but we haven't lost anything."

The man looked uncomfortable. "Well, some people sort of mentioned, not accusing, you understand, that big dog of hers."

"Cougar?" Matt laughed. "He'd never hurt a fly, unless it was hurting Alex."

Howard shifted his feet and didn't meet Matt's eyes. "Well, that's what I told him—"

"Who?" Matt asked.

The deputy's head came up. "Well, now, I couldn't exactly tell you that."

Matt looked at the man narrowly. "Doesn't Alex have a right to know who's running around accusing her dog of things like that?"

"Sure, but—"

"Who said it?"

They were the first words Michael had spoken, and something in his tone made the deputy meet his eyes. The man swallowed, looking as if he wanted to turn away but couldn't.

"Who?" Michael repeated softly.

Howard stared as if mesmerized, and when he spoke, it was as if the words were being dragged from him.

"Willis," he said slowly.

Michael's brow furrowed as he reached for the memory, knowing he'd heard the name somewhere.

"Henry? He's the one who said this?" Matt sounded not at all surprised.

Then Michael had it, the image of Alex mentioning the Mr. Willis who ran the gas station where they had encountered the grumpy bank president.

"Not exactly," Walt was saying. "He just said it would take an animal the size of that dog to bring down those calves and sheep." He coughed and, looking decidedly ill at ease, muttered something, then climbed back into the marked car and started the engine.

"Is he talking about the guy who owns the gas station in town?" Michael asked as he watched the car drive off.

"Not Pete. He's okay. It's his son. Henry." There was the slightest sour emphasis on the name.

"You sound like you don't like him much."

Matt grimaced. "Don't mind me. I don't care for a lot of people around here. Only came here because of..."

He trailed off, and Michael read the look in his eyes easily; pain, sadness, and regret rose in a swamping wave.

"Gary Swan?" he finished quietly.

"Yeah. Gary."

"You knew him pretty well, didn't you?"

"Yes. He was in my unit 'in country.' When I finally decided to get my life together, one of the first things I did was come here to see his father." Matt's eyes went oddly distant. "I was there when he died. I thought his father might want to know about it."

Michael reached out and touched Matt's arm gently. He maintained the contact, watching Matt's face until the far-off, haunted look disappeared. Slowly, Matt's head turned, and the look he gave Michael was calm and slightly bemused.

"You all right?" Michael asked.

"Yeah." He looked puzzled. "I feel...strange. But good. I don't usually talk about that." He shook his head. "Anyway, that's when I heard about what Alex was doing." He smiled. "I already knew about her, though. Gary kept talking about this little pixie back home. Said keeping the world safe for kids like her was the only thing worth fighting for."

"He was right."

"Yes, he was. So, I came out here. For his dad, and to see how she'd turned out, for Gary, sort of." He looked puzzled, as if wondering why he was telling this man so much. He ended the story rather abruptly. "And I stayed."

Michael nodded slowly, then tried to gently nudge Matt back to the subject of Walt's visit. "I gather this...Henry is not one of the reasons why."

Matt shrugged. "I don't know him that well, but Alex has known him all her life. She...dislikes him intensely."

"Hates him?"

"Alex doesn't hate anybody. But Henry Willis is about as close as she'll ever come to it."

"Why?"

"I don't know. I've asked, but she won't talk about it. I get the idea it's a long-time thing, though. And that's good enough for me."

Was that the answer? Michael wondered. Was it some long-held grudge that was behind what was happening here? Was it aimed specifically at Alex, rather than the refuge in general? No, he thought. It couldn't be. Alex could never do anything to inspire that kind of hatred.

Matt was watching Michael thoughtfully. "Long-time thing," he repeated. "Like Alex and the deputy, there."

"What?" Michael snapped back to the present.

"He's been trailing after her for three, four years now," Matt said casually.

"Trailing after her...?"

"Yep. Ever since he got assigned to this part of the county. Asks her out at least once a week."

Michael turned to stare back down the road. "How...does she feel about him?"

"Oh, she likes him well enough," Matt answered, his eyes trained on Michael's face. "Kinda keeps him at a distance, though. But then, maybe that's our fault, for keeping her so busy here."

Michael's gaze went back to Matt but darted away quickly. He usually had no problem with people reading his thoughts, but his faith in the ones he worked for was a little shaky at the moment. Besides, the knot in his stomach was so big he was afraid anyone with eyes could see he was messed up.

"Now that you're here to help, maybe she'll have more time free for him."

Michael jerked, his gaze snapping back to Matt's face; it was blandly innocent. "Right," he muttered, and stalked back to the barn, uncharacteristically unaware of Matt's grin behind him.

He went back to pounding nails into the crossbar with much more force than was necessary. What was wrong with him? He'd just been handed the answer to his dilemma. He knew Alex was becoming too attached to him, and what better way to solve the problem than by finding someone else for her?

He slammed the last nail home with a single furious blow.

Michael yawned despite the steady flow of chatter at the table; he'd spent a long, restless night. Sleep had eluded him in this place that seemed to echo hollowly, devoid of the bright spirit that made it live. Alex.

He'd spent the dark hours wondering if things were going as planned and what she was doing. Except for the frequent moments when he felt a soft, warm breath of air against his skin and knew what she was doing: she was thinking of him.

He'd tried to smother his chaotic feelings, but it was impossible in this place. In the hour just before dawn he had at last gotten up and made his way down the hall to her room. Cougar, sprawled disconsolately on the floor beside the bed, had raised his head to look at him, then lowered it with a heartfelt canine sigh.

"Yeah," Michael had muttered.

He'd sat down on the edge of the bed. Even here, where her presence was so strong, it felt empty. The way this house felt empty. The way he felt empty.

One hand had crept up toward the tags on his chest. He had to know what was happening, why were they letting it happen. But before his fingers reached the tags, they'd curled back against his palm. He'd sat there for a long, long time, only slightly comforted by Cougar when the dog got up and laid his big head on Michael's knee.

He'd nearly jumped when they'd called him.

*Michael.*

He grabbed the tags angrily. What?

*No need to sound so testy, Michael. You promised regular reports, remember.*

Fine. Here.

He sent them what he had, again edited.

*Thank you. You're doing fine.*

Sure I am.

*Something bothering you, Michael?*

I'm tired. You want twenty-four hour service, you should have fixed it so I wouldn't get tired.

*We tried. It would have been much more practical if you didn't have to rely on sleep, or food. But, unfortunately, there are some things that even we can't arrange.*

Pity.

*You seem to be awfully cranky on this case, Michael. Are you sure there isn't something wrong?*

Everything is just peachy. Good night.

He dropped the tags and shut his mind to them. And he'd spent the rest of the minutes before light began to fill the room wishing he could shut his mind to the images of Alex as easily.

And now he yawned again, pushing the remains of his dinner around on his plate. He was contemplating the glass of milk—part of the regular deliveries that had begun, unannounced, from Frank Morgan's small dairy farm—when a sweet, honeyed warmth began to spread through him. His head came up, tilting to one side as he stretched for the heat. Then he had it, and he couldn't help the smile that spread across his face.

"Hey, Mike, what's with you? You look like somebody just left you a million bucks."

He looked up at Steve and shrugged. "Nothing."

He turned his attention back to his meal, appetite a little stronger now. He had finished the last of his milk when they heard Cougar's joyous howl and, moments later, the sound of Alex's truck.

As they all poured out the door, Matt flipped on the outside light, casting a bright, golden circle into the yard where Alex had pulled to a halt. She seemed to hesitate inside the cab for a moment, and Matt went to pull open the door with a flourish.

"Welcome back, kid," he said melodramatically, bowing as she at last slid out and into the golden circle of light. "We missed—"

His words broke off sharply, and a muffled gasp rose from the rest of them as they stared at her. But Alex looked for only one pair of eyes. Bright, glowing, sky blue eyes. She found them, and they didn't let her down. More than just appreciation of her appearance, they held a teasing glint of "I told you so" and, without a trace of conceit, the fact that he had known it all along. The rest was hidden, locked away from her, but she was too excited to mind just then.

"Wow," Wheezer finally said.

"Yeah, wow," Steve echoed.

"Beautiful," Mark said gruffly, and Rick stood there staring as if he'd never seen her before.

Alex blushed, but she was pleased with their reactions. Her hair had been trimmed and shaped into a smooth, neck-

length sweep, tucked demurely behind one ear and falling
sexily instead of raggedly over her other eye. Long, lacy gold
earrings dangled from her ears, accenting the delicate lines
of her jaw and neck. The minimum of makeup, skillfully
applied thanks to a couple of hours of practice, highlighted
her cheekbones and the thick fringe of her lashes.

She'd found the dress she wore, a smooth, graceful knit
that accentuated her slenderly curved figure without clinging, in a small shop in the hotel. She'd fallen in love with it
immediately, especially when she'd tried it on and seen how
the deep jade color made her eyes stand out with startling
vividness.

She had sadly gone to put it back on the rack, knowing its
price was far out of her reach, when the clerk had come to
her, wearing the oddest expression, and told her it should
have been on the half-price rack. Alex had crushed her
qualms and bought it before her conscience could talk her
out of it. And also the matching pair of shoes that she had,
with incredible luck, found the same day in a small shop a
few blocks away. They were high-heeled and utterly im-
practical, and she loved the way they accentuated her legs in
their unfamiliar, sheer hose. She felt deliciously feminine
with the soft skirt swirling about her knees and the delicate
gold earrings dancing against her neck. Kid sister, huh? She
laughed inwardly.

"Well, are you going to let me come in? I have presents
for everybody."

She reached back into the truck and brought out a large,
gaily colored shopping bag. Matt scrambled for her small
suitcase as Aaron hastily went to hold the door open for her.

"You were supposed to spend that money on yourself,"
Aaron said sternly.

"Oh, I did, mostly." She laughed. "But it seemed like
everything I wanted was on sale. Now, sit down, all of you."

With all of them there they were short of seating, so Mark
lowered himself to the floor. Michael sat on the hearth,

where he busied himself starting the fire to ward off the evening's chill.

"Where's Cougar?" Alex asked.

Aaron coughed, and Matt looked uncomfortable.

"He's in the barn," Michael said quickly. "There's been some livestock killed, and I thought he'd be safer there until they find out what's doing it."

"Oh." A troubled line appeared between her brows.

"Don't worry about it now, Alex."

"Yeah," Matt chimed in hastily, managing to sound like a little boy on Christmas morning. "What did you bring?"

Alex smiled. "Sarah, you first," she said happily as she drew out a bright silk scarf in shades of gold and yellow that did wonders for Sarah's pale blond hair and caramel-colored eyes. Sarah exclaimed in delight; such things had long been beyond their limited budget. Mark crowed with pleasure as he opened the headphones she had given him so he could listen to his music anytime without disturbing the others. A stack of paperback mysteries went to Wheezer, who had a weakness for them, and a huge bag of gourmet jelly beans to Kenny, whose sweet tooth was legend. For Matt, a frustrated photography buff, came a book on the subject, and for Aaron a psychology text he'd been lusting after for months.

She hesitated for a moment, then reached into the bag again. She drew out a small, slim volume and walked over to Rick.

"I wasn't sure what you'd like," she said shyly. "But I know you were in the First Cav, and this was written by a First Cav captain. I thought they were wonderful. I hope you like them."

Rick stared at the book of poetry she held out to him, then looked back at her. His expression was very odd, and his voice more so as he at last moved to take the book. "I...thank you."

Michael looked up at his tone. For the first time the man's guard was down, and he could see what he needed to see.

Whatever was going on around here, Michael didn't think Rick was behind it. Rick was merely what he appeared: a haunted man with a scarred soul who was trying to heal. Michael turned back to the fire, adding another stick of kindling as he narrowed his list of suspects once more.

Alex went back to the bag one last time, conscious of everyone's eyes on her. They seemed to have an inordinate amount of interest in this last gift, she thought wryly. She lifted out the four-inch square box and carried it over to the fireplace. She sat down on the hearth and carefully put the box down between them.

Michael looked up, startled. He wasn't one of the group here, not really; he hadn't expected her to buy him anything. Then he met her eyes, and he knew that she had spent more time and care choosing this than anything else. That knot in his gut tightened another notch. He stared at the box for a moment. Then, with a hand that was none too steady, he reached for it.

The box opened to reveal a base of rough, jagged pewter. Atop it sat a three-inch crystal dragon, its tail curved into a flaring arch, each scale on its body cut in exquisite detail.

He reached out a tentative finger and touched the tiny beast, sensing through the polished facets that were flashing in the flickering light of the fire exactly what had gone into her choice of this gift. That knot leaped from his stomach to his throat, and Michael found himself blinking rapidly at the sudden stinging in his eyes.

Alex watched him a little breathlessly. She'd had no practice in this kind of thing; she only knew that when she'd seen the little crystal dragon she'd had to get it for him.

"Is it . . . all right?" She hated the way she sounded, but she couldn't help it.

He looked up then, and she saw the sheen of moisture in his eyes; he didn't try to hide it. "It's perfect," he said softly.

He meant it. He wasn't supposed to care about things; they weren't supposed to mean anything to him. That made it easier for him, they said. Well, if this was easy, he didn't want anything to do with hard. And to hell with their little rules; this tiny crystal creature was going to stay with him for a long, long time.

"We may have lost the little sister we all adopted," Aaron was saying softly, "but we gained a beautiful, extraordinary woman."

"We've taken you for granted for far too long," Matt added. "But not anymore."

Mark suddenly rose from the floor and engulfed her in a hug. "Beautiful inside and out, Alex."

Michael was still awake in his narrow bed when the rain started. He hadn't even tried to close his eyes, knowing that sleep would evade him again. Last night it had been because the house was so empty of her; tonight it was because the house—and his heart—were so full of her.

He'd always seen the beauty hidden behind the tomboyish exterior, but her transformation had stunned even him. She had been radiant in the rich green dress, alive with a newly discovered femininity. A femininity that called to something so deeply buried inside him that he wasn't even certain what it was.

He turned his head restlessly on the pillow, his gaze coming to rest on the tiny dragon on the table beside him. It seemed to glow even in the darkness, to sparkle with an inner light. He stared at it until the morning light, turned gray by the pouring rain, came through the window.

The rain kept on, as if trying to make up for its long absence all at once. By late morning they were stepping over rushing streams everywhere; by afternoon they'd given up on that and sloshed through the small rivers that crisscrossed the farm.

"Cougar's miserable," Alex said, listening to the dog's mournful howl as she helped Aaron spread a sheet of plastic over the chicken coop. "He hates being caged up like that."

"Mike's right, though," Aaron grunted as he secured one end of the plastic. "With whatever it is running loose killing livestock, he's better off locked in the barn."

Reluctantly agreeing, Alex moved to secure the other end. The dress had been traded for the necessary jeans, shirt, and boots, but the haircut remained, along with a slight touch of makeup and tiny gold earrings. She had, to her surprise, been able to hang on to the feeling her makeover had given her, in no small part due to the new way they all were looking at her. Maybe she wasn't forever doomed to be the world's little sister after all, she thought.

The downpour slackened to a gently steady rain by late afternoon, soft and pleasant. Chores done for the moment, Michael walked to the small clearing he'd found before. He found the spot soothing, and that was something he seemed to need a lot of lately. It was an unaccustomed feeling for him, and he didn't know how to deal with it.

He sat down for a moment, heedless of the wet ground and trying to think only of the clean, fresh feel of the rain on his face. The white-trunked alder tree offered scant shelter, often dousing him with larger drops that had collected on its round leaves, but he didn't care. The rain distracted him, although nothing seemed to keep his mind off a vibrant, slim girl in a clinging, tempting green dress.

Alex. God, what was wrong with him? How could she do it? How could she tie him up in knots like this? It had never happened before, not in all his years on the job, and he didn't know why it was happening now. Over the years he'd dealt with women who were, he supposed, more beautiful than Alex, and they'd had no effect at all on him. He'd wondered about it at first, that odd feeling not so much of something missing as something he should—but didn't—miss. Then he had come to realize the wisdom of it and to be thankful for the lack of emotional involvement. And now Alex had blown it all to bits, and he didn't know how.

At that instant she appeared, so quietly that he wondered for a moment if he'd discovered some heretofore unknown power to conjure up reality out of his own wandering thoughts. She seemed unaware of his presence as she walked slowly, her face turned up to the gentle rain. Michael could only stare at her, fascinated by the drops of liquid crystal lingering on her thick, dark lashes, by the fortunate raindrops that beaded on her skin and then darted downward, over her soft cheek, her delicate neck, down her silken smooth skin to disappear in the vee of her open-necked shirt just above the swell of her breasts. He wanted to follow that path, wanted to trace the rain's course with his fingers, with his lips, with his tongue. . . .

Alex turned sharply, and he knew she'd heard the sound he'd strangled in his throat. Quickly he tried to compose his expression, knowing that all his tangled emotions, all the untoward heat and hunger he was feeling, had to be showing on his face.

"You're getting wet," he said quickly.

"So are you."

She said no more, just looked at him, as if she knew exactly what he wanted. But she couldn't know, not when he didn't know himself, not when he didn't have the slightest idea why this was happening to him, or what to do to fight it. Or even if he wanted to fight it.

Did he? Or did he really, deep down, want to give up this battle he'd never expected to have to fight? The one they'd promised him he would never face? Didn't he want to throw it all away and forget the rules? Didn't he want to grab her and kiss her senseless, until they both went down like melting wax from the heat of it? Didn't he want to touch, stroke, and kiss every sweet inch of her, and—God help him—have her do the same to him?

He shuddered under the force of the images that swamped him then; he couldn't help it. He staggered to his feet. He had to get back in control, he thought grimly, feeling perilously close to losing his grip altogether.

"You'd better go inside," Alex said quietly. "You're shivering."

"Right," he muttered, but he wasn't about to argue with her, not when she was barely inches away, not when he could smell the sweet scent of her, could almost feel her skin beneath his fingers. Damn them, he ground out silently, why were they letting this happen? He made his way across the soggy ground to the house, every cell, every nerve ending in his body, aware that she was just behind him.

That night, their traditional evening spent around the fire in the living room seemed unusually short as one by one the others left for the bunkhouse, claiming weariness after a day full of work.

Michael knew what they were doing; he'd sensed their plot to leave him alone with Alex in this romantic setting, with a cozy fire inside and rain outside. He fought the urge to run, to avoid this, but when she sat down in front of the fire to dry her still damp hair, just a scant two feet away, he couldn't seem to move.

The light from the fire brought out the flames in her hair, the thick silk of it gleaming as she brushed it into the smooth cap of her new haircut. The sight of it, and the graceful movements of her arm as she lifted the brush, seemed to hypnotize him.

She stopped suddenly, looking up to find him staring at her. Her eyes widened, and her lips parted as she looked back.

"Michael . . . ?"

If he'd had more practice, he might have been able to resist the need that overtook him then. But in an instant he was back to where he'd been in the clearing, trying to battle something he had no weapons to fight, something that had never happened to him before, at least not in the memory they had left him. And when she looked at him, all wide-eyed and wondering, he never had a chance.

"Alex."

It came out on a gasping breath, and then she was in his arms. His mouth came down on hers hungrily, demanding the sweetness he'd barely tasted before. She yielded to him gladly, eagerly, her lips parting for his tongue the moment it flicked over them.

A low groan broke from him, and he pulled her hard against him as he plunged his tongue deep into the warm recesses of her mouth. He felt her move, felt her slender fingers tangle in her hair, heard the tiny sigh of pleasure she made as he crushed her mouth with his.

That sound ignited him, and his arms went tight around her as he took them both to the floor in front of the hearth. She was soft and warm and pliant beneath him, her fingers digging into the muscles of his shoulders as she clung to him. He deepened the kiss, probing, tasting, his head spinning with new sensations, his heart pounding a rapid cadence.

She moaned, her body rippling beneath him. He choked out a gasp as her breasts were crushed against his chest, then nearly stopped breathing altogether when her hips pressed against his. Involuntarily he jerked, grinding himself against her.

He realized then, through the haze, that the unbearable ache he'd been feeling was the unexpected, violent response of his body to the feel of her. His body was surging to life with a fierce swiftness that stunned him. He was hot and hard and ready, and he didn't know why.

He'd seen others in this state, although right now he couldn't believe he'd ever seen anything happen so hot and fast. He had even, at times, been part of bringing those people together. But he'd never experienced it himself, and he didn't know how to deal with it. He was way out of his depth, and with his last ounce of sanity he knew it.

"Alex," he gasped, lifting himself off her with a greater effort than he'd ever made in his life.

"No," she whispered, trying to pull him back, needing his heat, his mouth on hers.

"Alex, no," he choked out. "I can't. God, I can't."

He rolled away, his breath coming in short, sharp pants.
"Michael . . ."

"No!"

He jerked away from her outstretched hand, knowing that
if she touched him, he would be lost. Alex recoiled, paling
at his rejection. With a choking little sound she scrambled
to her feet, and without a word she ran out into the dark and
the rain.

"Alex!"

Michael struggled to get up, his body seeming to have
forgotten all its ordinary functions in the wave of new, unfamiliar sensations. He staggered to the window just in time
to see her disappear into the barn, Cougar at her heels.

He sagged back to the floor, propping himself against the
hearth, his back to the dancing flames. His body was
screaming; his mind was in turmoil. He had to have some
answers, and he had to have them now. This time, when he
reached for the tags, he didn't stop.

*My word, Michael, what's wrong? We've never heard—*

Get me the boss, damn it.

*Really, Mi—*

Shut up and get me the boss. I want some answers, and I
want them fast.

*But he's unavailable at the moment. He—*

I don't give a damn where he is. Get him.

A moment of silence. *Michael, are you in trouble? Please,
tell me.*

Even in his angry distress, Michael caught the difference.
Tell me. Not us, me. Except for the big boss, they never used
the first person. He must have rattled their cage. Or Alex
had, with what she'd done to him.

You're right, I'm in trouble. You said this would never
happen. You promised that it would never be a problem.
You even asked if I could handle it that way.

*Michael, please, calm down.*

Calm down? It's eating me alive, and you tell me to calm
down?

*What is?* It was nearly a shout, as close as he'd ever heard them come to an emotional outburst.

I love her, damn it!

Silence, stretching out, drawing his strained nerves even tighter. Then, at last, *Oh, dear.*

Oh, great. That's a lot of help. What the hell is going on up there, anyway?

*I don't know, Michael. This has never happened before.*

That doesn't make me feel any better.

*I can't answer you Michael. I'll have to find the boss.*

As I recall, that's what I asked for in the first place.

He knew it was bitterly sour, but he didn't care. Nothing mattered anymore except what was happening to him. And, more importantly, what was happening to Alex. He was hurting her, the very last thing he wanted to do. The very thing he'd been sent here to avert.

*Michael, please, just hang on. We'll find out, I promise.*

Right. Pardon me if I'm not real excited about your promises at the moment.

*I understand. Soon, Michael.*

And then they were gone, leaving him to fight the battle of his newly awakened senses alone.

# Seven

——

Alex shivered, but not from the cold. She was warm enough in her bed of straw, with Cougar beside her and Cricket above her radiating their body heat. She sat with her knees drawn up in front of her and her arms clasped around them, trying to control her shaking.

She'd done many things in her short life, she thought, but never had she so completely made a fool of herself. She'd thought she had herself under control, but when he'd looked at her like that she'd forgotten all of her lectures to herself at the first glimpse of the heat in his eyes.

On her trip to Portland, in the quiet hours alone, she had admitted, both fearfully and ruefully, that she loved him. She'd known it inwardly, although she had fought the knowledge, the moment she had seen him go down beneath that crashing, flaming beam. Her heart had screamed a protest that was immutable proof of what her mind had tried to deny.

She had also, in those hours alone, sworn that he would never know. That look of pain and guilt she had seen in his eyes when he had broken that unexpectedly hot and potent goodbye kiss had been seared into her mind, and she could think of only one explanation: he didn't want to hurt her. He knew the foolish little girl had fallen for him, and he was trying to be gentle. That was the kind of man he was, and she had sworn she would never put him in that position again.

So what had she done, within days of coming home? She had virtually thrown herself at him, practically begged him to kiss her. And he had. Oh, Lord, had he kissed her. She'd never known anything like that kiss, never felt anything like that total disruption of her senses.

Not that her experience was so great. There had only been a few chaste kisses from Walt Howard that had left her feeling a mildly pleasant warmth, nothing more. And that one, ugly experience that seemed so long ago that it could almost have happened to someone else. What had happened with Michael was so far removed from either of those that it was impossible to compare. Never in her life had she responded like that.

And it had affected him, too. Color flooded her cheeks as she remembered the rigid feel of him pressed so intimately against her. Surely that wouldn't have happened if he hadn't wanted her in return? Or was she being incredibly naive to think that it mattered, that it was her instead of just a willing female in general?

She didn't know. She almost laughed at the irony of it. She'd lived with anywhere from three to ten men at a time for the last eight years, been accused behind her back of everything from running some kind of sexual cult to indulging in one-woman orgies with all of them, and here she was at a total loss to understand one man's sexual reaction.

Some woman you are, she said to herself harshly. Can't even tell if a man wants *you* or just wants sex. Or . . .

Maybe that was it, she thought. He wanted it, but not with her. Not with her because he knew this was only a brief stop in his path, and he was too honorable to take her when he knew he would hurt her when he left, or...

Or he didn't want her, period. Much more likely, she thought bitterly. Just because she'd done as he said and discovered that she wasn't just the ragged little tomboy she'd always been didn't mean someone like him was going to fall at her feet. Sure, the guys had been bowled over by her new look, but they loved her already. Michael didn't. Why should he, when he could take his pick of all the women in the world?

In the end, she supposed, it didn't really matter. The result was the same, a deep, tearing pain that dug into some dark, protected corner of her soul.

"Oh, Cougar," she moaned. "What am I going to do?"

The dog lifted her head and licked her tear-stained cheek. She hugged him, burying her face in his thick fur.

Michael didn't know that it was already too late to avoid hurting her, she thought. He would be worried about that; he was too kind a man not to be. He would feel horrible if he knew how deeply she'd already been hurt, even though it was her own foolish fault. She could save him that, if she tried hard enough.

She would try. It would tear her up inside, but life had done that before and she'd kept on; she would do it again now. He deserved that much in return for all he'd done for them, if nothing else.

Tomorrow, she thought. She would begin tomorrow. Somehow she would face him as if this night had never happened. Tomorrow she would let him think it had meant nothing to her, freeing him from any responsibility he might feel. Tomorrow she would keep her head up and her eyes dry, no matter how much effort it took. But tonight...

Cougar whined his distress as his mistress wept dismally against him.

\* \* \*

As it turned out, it was easier than she'd expected. For two days Alex saw Michael only at meals. She had to make very little effort to avoid him; he didn't ever seem to be around, no matter where she was. Because he's avoiding you, she told herself acidly. What did you expect?

Therefore she found it curious that he appeared just as Walt Howard drove up to the house.

"Hi, Alex," Walt said with a fond smile, getting out to give her a hug.

"Hi, Walt."

She restrained her instinctive desire to pull away from him; Walt was her friend, and she wasn't going to let a foolish infatuation with a man who wanted nothing to do with her ruin that.

"You look . . . different." Walt backed up to look at her.

Different. Yes, she supposed that was all she had really accomplished. She just looked different. She was still that same naive country girl, just with a different wrapping. Michael had proved that to her quite thoroughly.

She was too aware of Michael's presence, and of the fact that he was watching them. She spoke hastily. "What brings you out here?"

"I wanted to let you know that a lot of people think it was a good thing you all did, helping the Morgans that way."

"Oh?" She smiled wryly. "I didn't think there was anything we could do that would impress Riverglen."

"Well, people are talking a little differently now."

Trying not to look at Michael, she lifted an eyebrow at Walt. "You came all the way out here to tell me that?"

"Not just that."

"What else, then?"

Walt coughed, then shifted his feet. "Why, to see you, of course. I thought you might have lunch with me."

"I can't," she answered automatically. "I have too much to do today. I have to clean up Cricket—he got so muddy after the rain—and I need to treat his feet. He's been standing in a lot of mud lately.''

"I'll do it," Michael said suddenly.

Alex flushed. "But I have to bathe Cougar."

"I'll do that, too. Go ahead and go."

Pain tore through her, but Alex set her jaw and brought her head up proudly. "All right."

Emotion flared in a pair of sky blue eyes—pain, resignation, and a spark of pride at her courage. None of it made any sense to Alex.

"Good," Walt said brightly. "And thanks," he added to Michael. "Oh, speaking of Cougar, you are keeping him tied up or inside, aren't you?"

"What?" Alex looked at him blankly.

"Well, we've had two more animals killed. Like I told Matt, I don't think he had anything to do with it, but there are still some rumblings going around."

"Cougar? Something to do with it?" Her eyes shot to Michael's face. "That's not what you told me!"

"You know it's not true," he said. "He's been locked up since—"

"Yes, but I had a right to know somebody thinks it is!"

"I . . . didn't want you to worry."

Alex was angry now. "How can I protect him when I don't know? I thought at least *you* weren't treating me like a child, but I guess I was wrong. I seem to be making a habit of it lately!"

Michael winced, and Walt spoke hastily.

"Alex—"

She whirled on him. "Who thinks Cougar did it?"

"Only one person, and nobody's really listening. It seems things are changing in town."

"But—"

"Let's go, Alex. We'll talk about it later."

Alex turned to look back at Michael; he was gone. Battling tears, she let Walt lead her around to the passenger side of his car.

Aaron stood watching Michael watching Walt drive away.

"Interesting, isn't it? Walt can't decide if he wants to pursue her or not, until the town begins to decide maybe we're not so horrible after all."

Michael clenched his jaw. "He's a decent guy."

"Sure," Aaron agreed easily. "Nice enough, if a little wishy-washy. When the town wanted her and us out, he was really careful about who knew he came to see her. Now, all of sudden he shows up to take her out in public."

Michael muttered something unintelligible and stalked off. When he got into the toolshed, he slammed down the plane he'd been using to fit the new barn door. His stomach was churning, and he had to bite back a string of angry, vicious curses. Nonchalantly sending her off with Walt Howard had ripped at him so fiercely he was surprised he wasn't bleeding. Maybe he was, inside, he thought grimly.

He didn't even bother to reach for the tags; he'd had no help or even contact from them since his last explosive message. Either they were giving him time to calm down, or they didn't know what was happening, either. Or perhaps they had abandoned him entirely, he thought suddenly. Was that what they did when somebody got out of line, put of synch? He'd done some things they hadn't totally approved of now and then, but he'd never gone completely haywire on them before.

What if they had abandoned him? He'd been working for them for so long, he didn't know anything else. What would he do? The answer came from someplace deep inside him, fully formed and definite. He would spend the rest of his life with Alex, trying to make up for being such a bastard to her. If, of course, they left him a life.

"Come on in, Mike," Matt called effusively. "You can help us ward off this disaster."

Alex looked up in time to see him hesitate in the doorway of the house. She and Matt and Aaron were at the small coffee table in the living room, some papers and a notepad spread before them.

"I just came back for my gloves," he said and started to walk past them toward the kitchen, where Sarah was washing the lunch dishes.

"Well, give us a hand anyway," Aaron said. "We decided to all go to the town meeting tonight. You know people, maybe you can come up with the arguments we need."

"You mean that Alex needs," Matt said. "She's going to have to do this." He put a hand on her shoulder. "Sorry, honey, but you're the only one they'll listen to."

Alex saw Michael look toward her, and she dropped her gaze to the notepad in front of her before their eyes could meet.

"You'll manage," Michael said tightly, then walked on into the kitchen.

Matt stared after him, then looked at Alex. "You two have a fight or something?"

Alex's grip on her pencil tightened. "What would we have to fight about?" she asked evenly.

Matt's eyes met Aaron's over her bowed head. They glanced toward the kitchen; then Aaron shrugged in disavowal of any understanding.

"Can we get on with this?" Alex asked a little sharply.

"Sure, I just—"

Matt broke off as two things happened: Michael came back in, tugging on his heavy work gloves, and as he passed it, the phone rang.

Michael nearly jumped. Aaron's eyes widened; he'd never seen Michael startled by anything. He must really be on edge, Aaron thought, his eyes flicking back to Alex's bowed head.

"Get that, would you, Mike?" Matt called out, and as Aaron's gaze lifted to Matt's face, he knew that Matt had sensed the same thing. And had asked Michael to get the phone on purpose, to keep him from leaving.

Michael knew he couldn't very well refuse, so he picked up the receiver. He answered, listened for a moment, spoke briefly, then hung up. The others were watching him, including Sarah, who had come in from the kitchen. He looked at her, at Matt, at Aaron, at everyone but Alex, as his words came out in short, choppy bursts.

"That was Mayor Barnum. There's a kid lost. Somewhere up in the hills above the east end of town. They figure he's been gone nearly fourteen hours."

"They figure?" Aaron asked.

"He snuck out last night. With a friend. The friend came home this morning. Said they got separated in the woods and he'd been looking all night."

"That's terrible!" Sarah exclaimed. Their only daughter was grown up and married now, but Sarah and Kenny had never lost their soft spot for children. "Poor child."

"Maybe," Michael muttered. And at last his eyes met Alex's. "It's Billy Peterson."

Alex held his gaze, although it took every bit of her will to look into those sky blue eyes and say evenly, "The sins of the father? I think not. He's still a boy." Her eyes flicked to Matt. "I'll take Cricket. I can cover more ground that way."

God, I love her, Michael thought. She's got more nerve and brains and goodness than anyone I've ever met. He had to look away; his faith in his ability to hide his thoughts from her was shaky beside the strength of his feelings.

Matt was speaking rapidly. "I'll get the truck. Aaron, round up Wheezer and Mark and Rick. Steve and Kenny aren't back from Eugene yet, though."

"I'll leave them a note," Sarah said, and hastened off to do so.

Alex watched them go, smiling softly. They'd never hesitated this time. They were becoming part of this community they had once held themselves so far apart from. And the community was accepting them at last. What she'd tried to accomplish in eight years had been done in less than a month. Thanks to Michael.

She realized then that he was still there, watching her. She tried to steel herself, to ignore him, but she couldn't deny him what he'd earned. She turned to look at him.

"Thank you," she said softly, hoping he would understand all she meant. The blue eyes lost their guarded look and went warm and soft with that inner glow, and she knew he had.

"Take Cougar with you," he said after a moment. Memory flashed in her eyes, destroying the momentary warmth and striking at him like a blow.

"I thought I was supposed to keep him tied up?"

He cringed inwardly at the memory of that day he had sent her off with Walt Howard, but he kept his expression even. "He might be able to help."

"Right."

She turned on her heel and left him standing there. He let out a long breath. He hadn't known it was possible to hurt like this. Or if he ever had, he'd forgotten. It was a moment before he could make himself move to join the others in the truck.

They easily found the makeshift command post Walt Howard had set up. Walt was speaking to the group of people gathered around his sheriff's unit.

"—haven't located the boy by dark, we'll call in outside help. There are trackers, dogs, and people trained in this sort of thing that we can call on. We'll find him."

Off to one side, Michael saw the woman from the store, Billy's mother, weeping in the arms of a heavy, ponderous looking man with a band of white skin above a tanned face, indicating he rarely went without wearing the rather grubby looking cap he held.

Michael stared at him, concentrating. He got the chaos of worry, anger, and frustration, the almost nauseating vibrations of a mean, shriveled spirit, but not the dangerous radiations of evil; he moved the man down lower on his evershortening list of suspects.

He still had his abilities, so they hadn't abandoned him after all, he thought in passing as he narrowed his focus, willing the man to turn.

"Uh-oh," Steve muttered. "Old man Peterson's spotted us. That won't make him happy."

"Nothing makes that man happy," Aaron said grimly. "But we make him particularly unhappy."

It was true, Michael thought, as he kept his eyes on the man. He was one of those who was not happy being happy. But although his eyes narrowed at the sight of them, the worry over his son outweighed his dislike, and he turned away without doing anything. Good, Michael thought. There was hope.

Alex rode up just as Walt spread a map out on the hood of his car. The young deputy gave her a smile, then handed her one of the whistles he'd been giving everyone else.

Michael caught a glimpse of someone on the edge of the crowd, someone whose attention was riveted not on the sheriff but on the group from the refuge. About the same age as Aaron and the others, the man seemed familiar somehow, yet he didn't recognize the face. He was tall, thin, and sallow looking, and something about him set Michael's teeth on edge. He looked at Aaron.

"Who is that?"

Aaron glanced toward the man. "Ray Claridge," he said shortly.

"Is he a local?"

Michael saw a muscle jump in Aaron's jaw but heard only a careful evenness in his voice. "Sort of. He grew up here, but he . . . left for several years. He came back a few years ago. Alex knows him better than I do."

Michael stared at the tall man, wishing he could make the connection. Under the force of his gaze, although that hadn't really been his intent, the man suddenly turned and moved away. Something in the way he walked struck home, and in that moment Michael knew where he'd seen him before. Dr. Swan's office. His gaze narrowed.

"Has he given you any problems?"

"No."

Michael sensed there was more, but before he could ask, Walt was giving directions and Aaron had turned to listen.

"We'll divide up the area to be searched. From what the other boy told us, we need to concentrate on that area, there." He gestured toward a thick belt of trees to his right. "We'll make the area between the river and the mill road one. I'll take that, along with the mayor's team."

Nice choice, Walt, Michael thought sourly. Run for office someday; you've got the moves. He turned to stare up at the low ridge that ran along the edge of town, concentrating, stretching, searching....

"Area two will be between the mill road and the start of the north ridge line. Sam, you and your group take that. Area three will be the ridge line. It will be tough, because of the terrain, so—"

"We'll take it," Michael said suddenly. All eyes shifted to him and the group of men standing beside him.

"That's rough ground," Walt began, glancing at Alex.

"We'll do it," she said. "I know the area, Walt, and so does Cougar. And Cricket. And the guys can handle the terrain."

After a moment Walt nodded. "The signal will be three long blasts on the whistle, all right?" They all nodded and began to scatter.

The men from the refuge clustered around Michael. He took charge so naturally, Alex thought. And they all listened to him, these gruff, war-toughened men who seemed to have forgotten they had ever doubted this man.

"Aaron, you and Rick start up the west boundary of this section," Michael said.

They both nodded, even Rick. Another transformation since Michael had come, Alex thought. Something cold seemed to squeeze her heart, but she forced it out of her mind.

"Mark, you and Wheezer take the section from the base of that rock up."

They looked over at the boulder he indicated and nodded. Michael knew he was dealing with men who understood searching unfamiliar country; they didn't need him to tell them how to do it. He paired himself up with Matt, then turned to Alex.

"I saved the best for you, Lexie," he said softly. "It'll be easier for you and Cricket to check the gorge trail."

She blushed at the nickname but only nodded, not taking time to wonder how he had managed to become so familiar with the countryside. The gorge trail was a narrow track that made its way up the ridge in a single straight line; it was steep but not necessarily treacherous if you took your time.

Alex whistled for Cougar and started off, ignoring the looks the big dog drew from some of the gathered crowd. If they were too blind to see the brave, fearless, honest heart of the big animal, it was their problem, she thought angrily.

They had been slogging through the brush-covered, still soggy landscape for nearly three hours when Michael suddenly came up short, his head cocked as if listening. Matt stopped behind him.

"What's wrong?"

It took a second for Michael to make the switch back to his actual surroundings. "Er, I'm a little tired. Let's take a break."

"You?" Matt chuckled. "Aren't you the guy who's been running me ragged all afternoon?"

"So I ran myself ragged, too." He found a relatively dry log and sat down. Matt followed suit gratefully, reaching for the canteen he was carrying for a quick drink.

Michael leaned back against an upthrust branch, closing his eyes. He let his surroundings slip away, let his senses expand, and after a moment he had it.

It unrolled against his eyelids as clearly as a piece of film. Cougar, ears suddenly upright, scampering off into the brush, Alex pulling Cricket to a halt on the trail, waiting. Then the excited barking of the big dog, and a faint wailing cry.

Alex wheeled the big horse on the narrow trail and sent him into the brush after Cougar. She shouted, and the cry came again, a little stronger this time.

Careful, Alex! Michael sent it to her on the wind, a sharp, short warning. His hands tightened into fists, relaxing only when she looked up, startled, and he knew she'd gotten it. Just in time, she pulled the paint to a halt. His hooves sent a little slide of rain-drenched soil down the sharp drop that loomed in front of them, hidden by a particularly heavy growth of brush.

"Down here! I'm down here!"

Cougar was barking furiously, and Alex listened, trying to judge how far down he was.

"Hang on, Billy! I'll be right there!"

She slid off the big horse and took down the rope that was fastened to the saddle. She looped the end over the saddle horn and tossed the rest over the drop. She yanked a pair of gloves out of her saddlebag and pulled them on, then took a brief moment to steady the horse.

"Easy now, love," she crooned. "Steady. Don't be dancin' around now, darlin'."

A mile away Michael smiled; she sounded like Andrew with his exaggerated drawl.

She went over the drop without hesitation, hand over hand down the rope, her boot heels digging into the damp earth. Cricket never moved; he stood like a statue of black-and-white marble, the only motion his ears as they swiveled, listening.

She found the boy wedged between a rock and a fallen tree, with Cougar crouched over him, licking his ear in an effort to comfort him. Billy's left ankle was twisted painfully, caught beneath a branch of the tree. A pair of frightened eyes in a dirty, tear-stained face widened when he recognized her, but surprise didn't stop him from clinging to her when she reached him.

"It's okay," she soothed. "We'll get you out of here right away."

She freed his foot, moving with exquisite gentleness when the boy cried out.

"I know it hurts, Billy, and we'll fix it real soon, but we've got to get up the hill first."

"I f-fell," he stammered. "The ground sl-slipped. And I was so c-cold."

"I know, Billy, but it's all over now. You'll be home in no time."

She had the rope secured around them now and sent a sharp whistle upward. "Cricket! Back, Cricket, back!"

The response was immediate as the well-trained stallion began to move, his muscled hindquarters breaking a pathway through the brush. Slowly, with Alex shouting encouragement, the big horse lifted them up the steep slope as Cougar raced up and down, barking excitedly.

"That's it, Billy, we're okay now," she told him as they came up over the top. She called to Cricket, and the horse's black-and-white head soon poked through the brush. She got the first-aid kit she'd stuck in the other saddlebag and quickly taped up the boy's injured ankle. Only then did she think to reach for the whistle around her neck and give the signal.

"There," she said soothingly as the echo of the whistle faded away. "Now your folks know you're found. Let's go home, okay?"

She helped him up into the saddle, cradling his sore ankle until he was settled. She was about to climb up behind him when he spoke, soft and wondering.

"You came after me."

"Of course."

"But I was so mean to you, I said those things—"

She stopped then and stood looking up at him. "I won't say it didn't hurt, Billy, because it did. Lies always hurt someone. But you're still young, and maybe you don't know any better yet."

"I'm sorry."

A tear trailed down his grubby cheek. He bore no resemblance to the cocky boy she had seen in the store that day; now he looked like what he was, a frightened child.

"Just remember that next time you feel like calling somebody names."

"I will," he promised fervently. Alex mounted behind him and held him carefully as they started down the hill.

"Michael! Wake up, man! Didn't you hear the whistle? They've found the kid."

Michael's eyes opened slowly. "Yes," he said softly. "I know."

Most of the searchers were back by the time the big paint horse came walking out of the woods. Mrs. Peterson gave a glad cry and ran forward, her smile changing her entire appearance. Her husband followed more slowly, joy lighting his face, but confusion in his eyes, the confusion of a man feeling a tremendous gratitude toward someone he didn't want to like.

"Cougar found me, and Alex came right down the side of the cliff. She was awful brave! And then Cricket pulled us up—"

Billy was engulfed in his weeping mother's arms as Alex helped him slide out of the saddle.

"Careful," she cautioned. "His ankle is hurt. It might be broken."

Myra Peterson looked up at the woman on the horse, her eyes still streaming. "Bless you. I don't know why you did this for us, we've been . . ." She faltered and hugged Billy even tighter.

Her husband laid an unexpectedly gentle hand on his son's head, then looked at Alex as she slid off Cricket's back.

"Thank you for my son." he said gruffly, holding out his other hand. Alex took it without hesitation.

"You're welcome," she said. "I'm glad we could help. But you'd better get him over to Doc's, to look at that ankle."

"Wait!" Billy cried. "I want to thank Cougar."

At the mention of his name the big dog scampered up to the boy and began to lick his face sloppily. Billy giggled and threw his arms around the shaggy neck; the animal fairly wriggled in delight. Alex was aware of the looks coming from several among the gathered townspeople—the ones who had suspected the big dog of the murderous livestock raids, she guessed—but her eyes stayed on Billy as he looked up at her.

"Do you think I could come and play with him sometime?"

Alex knelt beside the pair. "I think he'd like that," she said solemnly. "As long as it's all right with your parents."

"Can I Mom? Dad? Please?"

"Well . . ." George Peterson began doubtfully.

"I have to, Dad! Alex might never have found me if Cougar hadn't found me first!"

"Of course you can," his mother said suddenly, unexpectedly. "But now you need to go see Dr. Swan."

Billy made a face. "But I can't walk, Mom," he said, looking at the clinic about a hundred yards away.

"Carry you, if you want," Mark said.

Billy eyed the big, bearded man warily. But when he saw how Cougar rubbed up against the big man's leg, and the way Cricket nuzzled him familiarly, he nodded suddenly.

"Okay."

George Peterson looked as if he wanted to protest, but his son was too big for him to carry, so he subsided. Mark lifted him easily, cradling the boy carefully against his broad chest.

"Wow!" Billy exclaimed. "You're really tall!"

"You too someday."

Billy's eyes widened. "You think so?"

"Don't fall off mountain anymore," Mark said sternly.

Laughter rippled through the onlookers. Genuine, friendly laughter, not the rude, contemptuous sound Mark had been subjected to so many times before. He knew the difference, and when a smile split his bearded face, it transformed him. Alex surreptitiously wiped at her eyes; she loved that big man dearly.

"Atta girl, Alex!"

"Way to go!"

The cries rang out from all through the crowd as Mark carried the boy into the clinic. Alex smiled a little vaguely.

"Good work, Alex," Walt slipped an arm around her. "How about dinner tonight? The biggest steak in town for our heroine."

"No thanks, Walt. I appreciate it, but all I really want is a long, hot bath. I have to be back for the town meeting tonight."

"Another time then." Walt seemed to accept her refusal gracefully and left to go back to the milling group. Alex turned to remount Cricket and head home but stopped when a furtive movement from behind the clinic caught her eye. She saw who it was, and her mouth twisted with distaste.

"Alex? What is it?" Michael had appeared suddenly, but she was too tired to be startled.

"Nothing." She reached past him for the stirrup.

"Who was that?"

"Henry Willis."

Michael wheeled around to stare, remembering what Matt had told him, what Walt had said about the man's insidious suggestion about Cougar. Alex took advantage of his movement to swing up into the saddle.

"What is it, Alex?" Michael asked at last. "Why do you dislike him so?"

If she hadn't been so tired, she never would have said it. But she *was* tired, physically and emotionally. The intensity of the search had drained her. She'd been battered by Michael's rejection and her own uncertainty, and the specter of the threat to the refuge that hung over them tonight. Her guard was down, in tatters, and it slipped out.

"No big reason," she said acidly. "I just don't care for so-called men who molest children."

She whirled Cricket and put her heels to him, leaving Michael staring after her in shock.

# Eight

———

The church auditorium that was used as the town hall was filled to overflowing. Alex nervously smoothed down the skirt of the simple, button-front dress she'd worn. She had been to a few of these meetings, but never had she seen so many people at one. Did it have something to do with them? she wondered. Did so many people still hate them, that they had joined together to try and get them out?

Alex turned to look at Aaron, needing the reassurance of the wiry, kind man who had been with her since the beginning. Instead she found Michael sitting next to her, and she drew back in surprise.

She had refused to talk to him after leaving him that afternoon, already regretting what she'd said. He'd tried to get more out of her, knocking on the bathroom door while she was cleaning off the remnants of her trip down the side of the ridge, and later on the bedroom door after she'd locked herself in. She'd ignored him, although it had more than once taken her teeth clamped on her lower lip to do it.

When they had gathered to leave, she had taken refuge in the middle of the group and gratefully accepted Aaron's offer to drive her in his little convertible. He put up the worn top and handed her in as if it were a chariot; Alex felt more like it should have been a jeep, carting the losing general off to the battle.

"It's going to be all right," Michael said softly.

She tried to look away, but his eyes drew her with that odd power that she couldn't seem to resist. It filled her again, that calm peace, that feeling of security, and she wondered how it was possible for him to make her feel this way at the same time that he was tearing her apart.

"Ahem, ladies and gentlemen." Mayor Barnum had taken the dais and was tapping the podium with the gavel. "I have an announcement to make. In view of the events of this afternoon, it has been moved, seconded, and passed in chambers that this meeting be limited to only one item of business tonight."

Alex's shoulders sagged; she hadn't wanted to do this at all, but she had been set for it tonight and didn't look forward to having it drag on for another month.

"That one item was also passed unanimously. It is, in short, an acceptance of the voluntary withdrawal of a complaint requesting an investigation into a possible zoning violation."

Alex's head shot up. Mayor Barnum was looking straight at her and smiling.

"I think today—this past week, in fact—has proved quite clearly that Alex Logan and her friends are a part of this community. A valuable part. And I thank Mr. Peterson for withdrawing his complaint."

All their heads swiveled around toward the red-faced man who sat off to one side.

"And with that I declare this meeting adjourned!"

A round of applause broke out around the room, and a dazed Alex was enveloped in congratulatory hugs.

"How about that?" Aaron crowed.

"All right!" Matt laughed.

"Safe now," Mark said, practically lifting her off the floor with his embrace.

"Let's go celebrate!" Steve exclaimed.

Alex shook her head. "You go," she said numbly. "I'm going home." She tried visibly to steady herself, then looked at them all. "Don't thank me," she whispered. "Thank Michael. He did it."

Aaron nodded slowly, then grinned. "Uh, unaccustomed as I am to public speaking," he began with a laugh, to a round of boos and hisses. "Seriously, there is something I wanted to say. Something happened tonight that has never happened since Alex started the refuge. This town made an overt gesture of friendship to us. And I think it's clear to all of us that we have one person to thank for it."

They all nodded.

"So," Aaron went on. "From all of us, thank you, Michael. You shamed us into doing what we should have been doing all along."

"You just needed a nudge in the right direction. You've all been fighting for so long, you forgot how to make peace."

A strangled little sound broke from Alex. Then she whirled and ran toward the door, although her progress was impeded by several newly gained well-wishers. The others turned to look at Michael, who was watching her go, looking oddly pale. He took a hesitant step, as if to start after her, then stopped.

"Here," Aaron said, holding out the keys to his precious convertible. "Go take her home. She's wiped out. We'll get home in the truck."

Michael stared for a moment; then, as Alex finally made it out the door, he grabbed the keys and ran.

He was surprised that she didn't fight him until he took her elbow to help her into the little car. He realized then that she was utterly drained, like a soldier who had drawn on the

last of his reserves for the fiercest fight and then found it was
over before it began.

He started to lower himself into the driver's seat when a
chilly blast of air struck the back of his neck. The gust startled him, since there was no wind tonight, but when he
whirled around to look, he thought he understood. For
there in the doorway of the auditorium, standing next to the
tall, gangly figure of Ray Claridge, was Henry Willis.

He was torn for a moment, but the chance to probe at his
prime suspect seemed insignificant compared to the need to
get Alex home. He turned away and got into the car.

She said nothing all the way home, and nothing as they
went inside. She stopped in the living room doorway, while
Michael went to build up the fire, stoking it gently until it
was crackling, sending waves of heat into the room. They
needed a heat pump to recirculate the heated air, he thought.
Or a wood stove designed for heating. It would keep the little house much warmer with less wood.

He turned to see her still standing in the same spot, her
hands clasped tightly in front of her chin. They were trembling.

He crossed the room and swept her up into his arms. She
made a tiny sound of protest, but there was no force in it,
and he ignored it. He carried her to her bedroom and set her
down on the bed as he flicked on the light.

"No," she murmured as he knelt to slip off her shoes, but
her voice, too, held no conviction.

"Shh," he murmured. "You need to rest, Lex. That's all,
just rest."

He clamped on controls he'd never had to use before
when he began to unbutton the pale green dress. Controls
that slipped several notches at once when the dress slipped
off her slender shoulders and revealed a skimpy swath of
emerald green silk beneath.

He sucked in his breath. He'd been prepared for practical underwear—all, he was sure, she had ever been able to
afford. This was a stunning, breath-stealing surprise, this

silky, sexy little teddy. She must have bought it in Portland, he thought, and tonight she had needed the way it made her feel.

He knew he was trying desperately to keep his mind on things like that, to keep it off of how incredibly beautiful she was. Gone was any trace of the shaggy tomboy. This was a slim, lusciously curved, long-legged woman, with a burnished sweep of russet hair and a pair of wide green eyes that looked bottomless in the faint light from the bedside table.

"You need rest," he muttered harshly, more to remind himself than to convince her. It was the hardest thing he'd ever done to leave her there.

He was still wide awake, battling the resurgence and unfamiliar hardness of his body, when the phone rang. He'd heard the men and Sarah come home, their off-key singing telling him that the celebration had been a success. He'd tried to sleep, but, as it had done so many times before, it had eluded him. When the ring finally came, he knew he'd been expecting it.

He sat bolt upright before the echo died away and was on his feet, pulling on his jeans, before the second ring was cut off as she answered. He didn't wonder if it was the phantom caller again; he knew. He stopped at her closed door, spreading his fingers on the wood, closing his eyes.

"...Think you're set now, don't you, bitch? Got the town eating out of your hand now, right? All your problems are over?" A string of filthy, crude words followed. "They're just starting, slut. We haven't all been blinded by a few good deeds. You'll leave, and you'll be sorry you didn't listen to us before."

She said nothing, just hung up the phone with a quiet care that said a great deal about her state of mind.

"Alex!"

Nothing. He tried the door; she'd locked it.

"Alex, let me in!"

"No."

"Damn it, Alex—"

"Go away."

He hesitated, glancing at the tags that hung against his chest, but he didn't expect any help. They generally left him alone to do what he had to, but they'd never been this absent before. He took a breath, clenched his jaw and put his hand back on the knob. He stared at it, then tightened his grip until he heard the quiet click. It turned, and the door swung open.

Alex jerked upright. "I... I locked that."

"It didn't catch." He strode across the room and sat down beside her. "I know it was him, Alex."

"I... it doesn't matter. They're just phone calls."

Just phone calls. From someone who knew enough to call at night, knew that she was generally in the house alone then, knew that she would be the one to answer the phone. But he didn't say it; she was frightened enough already, no matter how bravely she tried to deny it.

"Alex—"

"Please," she whispered, shivering. "I don't want to talk about it."

"Alex, please. I know I've hurt you—"

"Not your fault," she said quickly, through teeth that were chattering. "I should have known better."

He felt her chill and moved to hold her. She tried to pull away, and he slid up beside her on the bed to stop her.

"Know better than what, Alex?" he asked softly.

She sagged, giving up the protest she didn't have the strength to make in the first place. "Than to think you might... want me."

"Oh, God, Alex," he said on a shuddering breath. "I do. I can't, I shouldn't, it's crazy, but I do. But—"

"No. Please. Just... leave it. I understand."

He wanted to explain, to tell her, but he couldn't find the words. He was having trouble just breathing, with her so close in his arms in that shimmering little thing that did so little to conceal the full curves of her breasts.

He wondered if the boss was blocking him, knowing how close he was to breaking the most important rule ever laid down for him. He thought it might be true, for the other words came easily enough.

"Tell me about Henry Willis."

She twisted in his arms, but he didn't let her go. "I shouldn't have said anything. It was a long time ago, and it doesn't matter anymore."

"Tell me." He lifted a finger to tilt her chin back and made her meet his eyes. "Tell me, Alex."

She shuddered, dropping her head as soon as he released her. He pressed her face to his shoulder, knowing the truth would come now.

"It was after my parents were killed," she said slowly. "I felt so... lost. Andrew tried to help, but he was hurting as much as I was. I started going for long walks. It helped a little. I ran into Henry one day, fishing down at the river."

She drew a shaky breath before going on. "He started hanging around, walking with me. He was older, twenty-five then, but I didn't realize it was a little strange that he had so much time for a fifteen-year-old. He seemed nice about it. He listened to me and never said much. I thought he was... trying to help."

She trembled again, and Michael pulled her around so that he could slip his other arm around her, too, to hold her more securely against the tide of ugly memories.

"One night...it was after Andrew had a really bad day...I had to go get a tire fixed at the gas station. Pete was gone, but Henry was there, and we talked for a while. But when I tried to leave..." She bit back a sob.

"Let it out, Alex," Michael whispered. "You've held it in for so long."

"He...grabbed me. I didn't realize what he was doing at first, until he threw me down on the floor and started ripping my shirt. Then he... hit me."

Michael fought back the tide of fury that rose in him; he had to concentrate on Alex now.

"I screamed, but he just laughed. He wouldn't stop. I tried . . . I clawed at him, I kicked, but he was so much bigger than me. . . ."

A twenty-five-year-old man against a fifteen-year-old girl. Michael was getting the images from her, broken, ugly pictures, ragged around the edges from being suppressed for so long in the innermost recesses of her mind. She'd had the memory buried so deep even his bosses hadn't found it. Fury surged in him again, and again he beat it back. He tightened his hold on her.

"What happened, Alex?"

"He . . . made me touch him. Through his pants." Her head came up then. "I did." The barest ghost of a smile flitted across her pale, strained face. "Hard. I got away then."

He got it then, the image of a slim girl fighting back the only way she could, with slender but strong fingers driving to do damage where it would hurt the most. Pride welled up in him, pride in her. He nearly laughed with the force of it.

"Oh, God, Alex, you're the most incredible woman I've ever known." He gathered himself when he saw her staring at him, wide-eyed. "You never told anyone."

Her eyes dropped to the quilt that was tangled around them now. "I couldn't. Henry knew that. It would have hurt Andrew terribly. He just would have felt even more helpless, knowing he couldn't even defend his little sister."

"So you carried it all alone, all this time."

"I just stayed away from him. And after Andrew died, I told him that if he ever came near me, or if I heard of him pulling that on anyone else, I'd go straight to the sheriff."

She saw Michael's eyes flick to the phone.

"No," she said slowly. "It can't be. He's left me alone for years now."

He wasn't sure, but he said nothing. He held her for a long time, whispering to her, telling her how brave and good and wonderful she was, softly blocking her automatic denials. She gradually relaxed and snuggled closer to him. He thought she had slipped into sleep when she spoke, in a tiny little voice that made a quiver run up his spine.

"Michael? Did you really...want me to go with Walt the other day?"

Oh God. "He's a good man, Alex."

"That's not what I asked."

"He's better for you."

"That isn't it, either."

"No. No, damn it, I didn't. I hated it. It shouldn't make one damn bit of difference to me, but I hated it!"

She moved then, sitting up so quickly it startled him. Her hair was tousled, her eyes wide as she looked at him. The covers dropped to her waist, and he could see the ripe swell of her breasts, the tips pressing tautly against the thin covering of emerald silk. His newly awakened body roused to the sight with a rush, and he groaned under the force of it.

"Alex . . ."

She lifted one arm, reaching out to lay her hand flat against his chest in the V formed by the golden chain.

"Alex, don't do this."

"You said you wanted me. . . ."

"But I can't—"

He broke off as, cheeks flaming, her eyes dropped to the zipper of his jeans and the unmistakable bulge behind it.

"God, Alex, you don't understand. This isn't right. Something's wrong, and I don't know what it is, but this shouldn't be happening."

"Why?" she asked in sudden fear. "Did you leave a wife behind somewhere?"

"No." He groaned again as her hand flexed on his chest, her fingers stroking his skin, sending heat out in rippling circles.

"It's all right," she whispered huskily. "I know that you don't... I don't expect anything."

"You should," he said harshly. "You should. You're too good for somebody who'll just move on, Alex."

A little stunned by her own boldness, Alex leaned forward. She knew what she was risking, knew that another rejection from him would shatter her fragile confidence. But she couldn't seem to care, and she bent to press her lips to his chest.

His muscles convulsed, his back arching involuntarily to press his chest against her mouth. In that second, when heat and sensation sizzled along every nerve in his body, he knew he was lost. It didn't matter anymore that this shouldn't, couldn't, be happening. The years he'd gone without feeling a thing didn't matter. It didn't matter what rules he was breaking, or what they would do to him. Nothing mattered except this woman and this moment.

He came up off the bed and rolled her beneath him. His mouth darted to hers, taking it hungrily, furiously, as if all those years alone had been damming something up somewhere inside him. She welcomed him, opened for him, and he drove his tongue into her sweet warmth.

Her arms went around him, and her nails dug into the muscles of his back as she clung to him, a low moan of pleasure rising from her throat. It coalesced into a breathy whisper of his name, and heat crackled through him like wildfire.

Her hands slid up his back to tangle in the thick hair at his nape. Her fingers caught the gold chain, and Michael's head came up suddenly. He moved a hand, caught the gold chain on one finger and tugged it over his head.

Alex watched him, her eyes puzzled.

"I don't want an audience," he growled, tossing the tags onto the nightstand.

Before Alex could even try to make sense out of that, his mouth was on hers again. She greeted his returning heat joyously, sending her own tongue daringly in search of his. They met, twirled, danced, and Alex felt herself shifting, changing, as if muscle and bone had melted into some golden, flowing liquid that was capable of feeling only pleasure.

Every touch expanded the heat; every movement of his body over hers made her less certain where the boundaries between them were. The solid wall of his chest crushed her breasts, and she reveled in it, arching herself against him to increase the pressure, twisting sinuously to rub her throbbing nipples harder against him.

Michael's breath left him in a rush, and he bore down on her with his full weight, wanting to feel every inch of her as she moved beneath him. He lowered his head and trailed a path of quick, hot kisses down the line of her jaw, the side of her throat.

Alex gasped, moaning his name again as his lips reached the high swell of her breasts. She'd never felt this, never known such a burning need. She felt the rippling movement of her body begin, the consecutive convulsions of muscles that had found a new purpose: bringing her body closer to his. Her hips, then her stomach, then her breasts, all arching, seeking, wanting him.

"Alex," he whispered thickly, "what are you doing to me?"

He slid his hands down her shoulders slowly, following his hands with his mouth. He was moving with a sureness that almost surprised him. He was vaguely aware of the fact that this was different, that this certainty was coming not from some source outside his own consciousness but from deep within him, from some long-forgotten place of ancient, primitive instinct that was rusty from disuse.

He moved to cup her breasts, and his body fairly sizzled as he lifted the full, feminine weight, as the soft flesh rounded into his palms. She gasped, lifting herself to him instinctively, and he couldn't resist the unspoken plea. His mouth went to one breast, his lips seeking, finding, the taut thrust of the tingling nipple beneath the thin silk. The sheer fabric was no barrier to his suckling kiss as he wet it with his tongue.

Her cry of shocked pleasure raced along his singing nerves. The crest tightened under his tongue, urging him on, and his body clenched fiercely around a white-hot shaft of need. He felt her hands slide down his chest to his stomach, and every muscle there contracted at her touch. Her fingers slipped down to his waistband to caress his belly. He groaned, low and deep, at the thought of what it would feel like if she moved her hand just a little farther.

He felt the sweet, hot pressure of her lips as she lifted her head to blaze a trail down his throat, lingering to flick her tongue in the hollow at its base.

He had to know. He had to feel her touch. He shifted his weight and gently grasped one delicate wrist. A throttled groan broke from him as he carefully moved her hand that last critical distance and pressed it lightly over the swollen flesh begging to be freed from the too-tight jeans.

He nearly gasped at the hot, brilliant flash of pleasure that shot through him. But he choked off the sound when he realized she had gone utterly still. Comprehension flooded him, and he let out a harsh breath as guilt rose up and kicked him in the gut.

"Oh, God, Alex, I'm sorry! I didn't think... Damn, and after you just told me what that bastard did."

"No," she whispered as she looked up at him, her eyes holding none of the fear, repulsion, or condemnation he'd expected. The green depths were full only of an awed wonder. "It's just... how different it is, how wonderful... when it's someone you love."

Her hand moved, flexed caressingly, and fire shot through him in a fierce burst. He shuddered, trying desperately to rein in his soaring senses, knowing she didn't even realize what she'd admitted.

She loved him. It didn't surprise him; he supposed he'd known it on some subconscious level for a long time. But it stopped him. He couldn't do this, not to Alex, not when she didn't truly know what she was doing.

God, it should be so easy! He loved her. She loved him. Hadn't he orchestrated this for others hundreds, maybe even thousands, of times? So why was it killing him, ripping him apart?

"Alex," he moaned, his head dropping to rest in the sweet valley between her breasts. "What am I doing?"

"Michael?"

She shook as his name escaped her, terrified that he was going to reject her once more. His head came up, and he took a long, slow breath as he looked at her.

"There's something I have to tell you."

"Now?" Her voice was tiny, strained.

"I have to. Before we…go any further. You have the right to know."

"You're scaring me, Michael. To know what?"

He reached for the tags on the nightstand. They glinted in the dim light. "Who I am," he said softly.

"But I know all I need—"

She jerked in response to the loud crack of sound, a startled cry breaking from her. Michael's head snapped around as they waited, frozen.

"That was—"

"—a shot. I know," Michael said grimly.

"Was it as close as it sounded?" she asked, trembling as she stared into the darkness.

"Afraid so."

He was on his feet and moving, tugging the gold chain and tags back over his head. He grabbed his socks and battered boots and yanked them on hurriedly as Alex tugged on her own jeans and boots. She reached for a heavy sweater, quashing a little pang as she pulled it down over the teddy that was still damp from his mouth.

The others were spilling out of the bunkhouse, and they met in the yard. They wasted no time on preliminaries; they all knew that hauntingly familiar sound too well.

"How far, you think?" Aaron asked.

"Hundred yards, maybe, depending on the gun," Matt answered grimly.

Michael nodded. "Up there, I think," he said, looking toward the hill behind the orchard. They nodded back.

"Where's Cougar?" Alex asked suddenly. The big dog had been nowhere in sight when they'd gotten home, she realized now. "Oh, God, what if somebody saw him out and thought he was—"

"Easy, Alex," Michael murmured. "He's in the barn. He was under house arrest until tonight, remember?"

Steve glanced around suddenly. "Mark's gone."

Michael's head came up sharply. "You're sure?"

Steve nodded. "I saw his bunk was empty. I thought he was already out here."

"We'd better find him." Wheezer said. "Let's each head—"

"No!" Michael snapped. "Nobody goes alone."

"He's right," Rick said suddenly, unexpectedly. "There's still somebody out there with a gun."

"Rick, Aaron, Steve, check along the road. Matt, you take Wheezer and Kenny and check the trees around the pasture. Then we'll all check the hill."

No one questioned his rapid orders, but Matt raised an eyebrow as he said, "That leaves you alone, Mike."

"I'll catch up. There's something I have to do first."

They hesitated, then went, as Rick reminded them of the need for haste. Alex stood stock still, looking at Michael.

"You're going alone, aren't you?"

He shrugged off her question. "Alex, listen. You've got to think. You know Mark better than anyone. Where does he go when he takes off like this?"

"Lots of places. Sometimes he just walks. It makes him feel better."

"What if he's already feeling good? Like tonight?"

Her eyes widened. "He goes to the rock," she whispered.

"The rock?" He looked over his shoulder and up the hill. "You mean the shelf up there?"

She nodded, not even wondering anymore how he knew about the big outcropping of rock that jutted out of the hill and gave an expansive view of the farm. Michael started off at a run but stopped when he heard her behind him.

"Stay here."

"Don't even start. I'm not sitting around waiting."

"Alex," he said tightly, "there's somebody out there shooting."

"Nobody goes alone. That's what you said."

He gripped her shoulders. "Alex—"

"I'll just follow you," she insisted.

He held her tight, staring into her eyes. Even in the dark she could see the warmth steal into the sky blue. "You are the stubbornest..."

Her chin came up defiantly. Michael laughed, hugged her swiftly, and said no more when she matched him stride for stride as he started up the hill.

They were about halfway up when the back of his neck began to prickle, the hair standing up as his muscles tensed. He looked around, but nothing moved. They kept on.

Ten yards later he stopped. Alex looked up at him questioningly, but before she could speak he held a finger to her lips and shook his head slightly. Then he backed up a step, lifting his head and closing his eyes.

"Michael?"

"He's still here. With the gun. I can feel it."

Alex paled. She never thought to doubt him; the certainty in his voice was undeniable. She shivered as they resumed the climb to the big rock that was Mark's favorite place, and it had nothing to do with the cold.

"Please," she murmured, not sure to whom. "Not Mark. He's been hurt so much already."

"I know, Lexie."

"All those years he was in the VA hospital...they thought that shrapnel had made him an...an idiot. And all it had done was damage his speech center. He was fine, his mind was fine, but he just couldn't talk to tell them."

"We'll find him, Alex."

"We have to. He's so special...and he's changed so much since the first week he came to us and realized he could talk the best he could and no one would laugh at him."

She couldn't stop the sharp, startled cry that slipped out when Michael whirled, then went rigidly tense.

"Him," he muttered, fury and realization in his voice.

He dived through the brush to their left. She followed, frightened but determined. He looked like a predator on the hunt, his eyes trained into the distance even though she knew he couldn't possibly see anything. Once, far ahead, she thought she heard another, heavier, clumsier movement, and her heart began to hammer.

And then he stopped. A short, muttered oath broke through the stillness. She came up hard against his back and staggered. She saw him give one last, angry look in the direction they'd been going; then he took two long steps to the right and went down on his knees.

Only then did she see Mark. Sprawled on his back, one hand on his chest, his bearded head thrown uncomfortably back.

"No!" Alex went down beside him, reaching for that limp hand. Then she drew her own hand back, staring at the ominous sticky redness. "Oh, God! Mark!"

Michael moved swiftly, his fingers feeling desperately for some sign of life. He found a faint, thready pulse, fading even as he felt it. "Damn."

*"No!"*

She shuddered violently as the word broke from her, and Michael saw in her eyes the crumbling of a valiant spirit. No, he echoed to himself. And he reached for the tags.

*Michael, we've been trying to reach—*

Later. This is more important. Mark's hurt. You promised he wasn't to get hurt.

*Yes, but—*

No buts. You're going to help me help him.

*Michael, you don't mean—*

Damn right I do. And right now.

*But the risk! If you fail, it could kill you both!*

Damn the risk. If I don't, he's dead for sure. There's no time to argue. You've blown a lot of promises lately but not this one.

*You're quite right. All right, Michael. Good luck.*

He caught a glimpse of Alex looking at him oddly as he dropped the tags, but he had no time to deal with her now. Every second mattered. He leaned over and gripped Mark's brawny shoulders.

Alex stared at him. She saw the change overtake him, saw him go pale, sweat beading up on his face and glistening in the dappled moonlight coming through the trees. His eyes closed, his face contorted sharply, and a hissing breath escaped through his clenched teeth.

When the first sound broke from him, Alex cried out his name. She'd never heard anything like it, never heard a sound so full of pure, burning agony. He was doubled over, his breath coming in short, choppy pants, the knuckles of both hands white with strain as he held on to Mark as if trying to lift his full, huge weight with just his fingers.

The sound came again, ripping, tearing. Then again and again, short, horrible chunks of sound. Tears streamed from Alex's eyes. She didn't understand what was happening, but she knew Michael was in agony. His beautiful face was twisted in such pain that it was almost unrecognizable. She was seized with a clawing fear that she was about to lose both of them, a fear that was a glowing hot blade slowly piercing her heart.

"Please no, please," she moaned over and over, feeling so utterly helpless that she wanted to cower and hide.

Suddenly Michael moved sharply, his lean body curling inward as a harsh, rasping breath burst from him. And then he went slack, like a puppet with all the strings cut at once. He crumpled, sliding off Mark's limp form and onto his back, the rise and fall of his chest so shallow that Alex was barely certain he was breathing at all. She just sat there, shaking, stunned beyond any understanding. Michael looked so pale, his skin almost translucent in the silver light, his eyes dark and bruised looking in his exhausted face. He looked, she thought in torment, as close to death as Mark.

Her eyes strayed to that beloved, bearded face. She reached out to touch his cheek, knowing she would find it cold and lifeless. And then, incredibly, Mark opened his eyes. And smiled at her.

# Nine

---

Michael felt the warmth, saw the light through his closed eyelids. Instinctively he turned toward it, tilting his head as if he could absorb some of the radiant energy. He needed it; he felt more drained and weak than he could ever remember.

He nestled into the pillow, wishing he had the strength to turn over and shut out the light so he could go back to sleep. But there was something he needed to do, wasn't there? No, it could wait. It had to wait. He was so tired, and just lying here felt so good. Too good. When had the narrow little bed become so comfortable?

He pried open one eye, then the other, then blinked at the flood of light. Alex's bed? He jerked himself up on one elbow, startled. And found himself looking right into a pair of emerald eyes.

Memory snapped back with a sharpness that was almost audible, sending weariness flying before the burst of adrenaline, like leaves before a hurricane. He searched her face, looking for some sign of what she was thinking. But for the first time he couldn't read her. The wide, innocent green eyes were shuttered against him.

Which told him what she was thinking, he supposed wearily, as clearly as if he *had* been able to read her. He sank back on the pillow. How many times had they told him? People didn't deal well with things they didn't understand, with things—or people—that weren't . . . normal. He had thought, had dared to hope, that Alex might be different. But it was too much to ask; it always had been.

He knew it wouldn't matter to her in the long run. The rule was only to make sure the job got done without interference, because in the end, when he left, it would all be taken care of. They would see to that. But he had hoped . . .

Had hoped what? For a miracle? He nearly laughed at the irony of it; he was in the business of making them, not getting them. A sick feeling, making his entire body ache and his gut twist violently, rose inside him.

Alex moved then, leaning forward in the chair she had pulled up beside the bed. Reflexively his eyes went to her, even though the last thing he wanted was to see that flat, shuttered look again.

"That was what you were going to tell me, wasn't it?"

Her voice was as expressionless as her face.

He let out a long, tired breath. Slowly, he nodded.

"Will you tell me now?"

Now. Now that she'd been frightened, repulsed by what she'd seen. Now that she knew he was not, in the usual sense, normal. He was different. Very different. Inhuman, from a human point of view. Desperately he tried to dodge what he knew was coming.

"Mark . . . ?" he began.

"He's fine." Alex looked at him steadily, as if she realized he was stalling. When she went on, it was in the short, clipped tone of a person getting a required report out of the way so she could get on to what she really wanted.

"Mark doesn't remember much. Or else he isn't saying. The guys got you both down the hill. I told them you fell getting to Mark. They put you to bed. Doc was here. He said Mark would be fine. He didn't understand how. He didn't understand what was wrong with you, either. He wanted you at the clinic for tests. I told him to wait. We were to call him if you didn't wake up by noon. Which is when he's going to call the sheriff. He has to, for any gunshot wound. But he gave us until then. Because I asked him to wait."

She'd handled it perfectly. She'd done everything he would have done, if he'd been able to. He let out a sigh as the weariness began to creep back into his body, into his very bones.

"Well?"

His eyes snapped open. The words, strained and tight, slipped out despite his efforts to stop them. "What's the point? You've already made up your mind, haven't you?"

"Yes," she said quietly, sending a dart of searing pain through a heart that wasn't supposed to be able to feel things like that. "But I still want to know."

"You want the whole story, right?" he asked bitterly.

"You told me I had the right to know."

The pain again, fierce, stabbing. "That was . . ."

He trailed off. The reason she had the right to know— because she loved him—obviously didn't exist anymore. It had been destroyed in a few desperate moments on a dark hillside. He was a freak now, something to be stared at, to be avoided.

"Help me understand."

For the first time a hint of emotion slipped into her voice. Michael drew a deep breath. Still he hesitated. But what did it matter? It was all going to be over soon anyway.

"Why not?" he muttered. "I've already broken every other rule."

"Rule?"

His eyes flicked to her again. Then he shifted, moving the pillows to prop himself against the headboard of the bed.

"Rules," he said at last, training his eyes on her. She looked so very vulnerable, huddled in the worn terry cloth robe she wore. He had to do this, he thought. He had to at least try and make her understand. She might not love him anymore, but he couldn't stand the idea that she found him repulsive.

"Whose rules?"

He began, speaking low and clear, using every ounce of energy he had left to will her into understanding.

"It started a long, long time ago, Alex. A group of ... people, for lack of a better word, stumbled across a place inhabited by a developing race of creatures they found fascinating. They saw potential there, and the seeds of disaster as well. For a long time they just studied those creatures, watching them change, grow. Sometimes not for the better."

She was listening, but he sensed the impatience in her.

"Stay with me, Alex. It's a long story." He realized his hands had curled into fists and consciously relaxed them. "These ... people, their own laws wouldn't let them interfere. But they found a way around that. They started ... recruiting people, people from this place."

"Michael, if this is supposed to be an explanation, it isn't working. I want to know about you."

He sighed. "All right, all right. Me." He took another breath. "It started in a coal mine. In Kentucky. There was an explosion and a cave-in. Twenty men died, the rest were dying. There wasn't any hope anyone would get there in time. The place was full of poisonous gas."

His eyes had gone strangely hollow. She saw a shiver ripple through him, and he took a quick, gulping breath, as if he hadn't been sure he could. Alex's eyes widened with realization; he had been one of those men. But before she could dwell on that, he was speaking again.

"One of those men who was left alive—barely—well, he started to hallucinate. At least, that's what he thought. A man seemed to appear in front of him. Just sat there, like there was all the air in the world. Then he offered the guy a way out. A job, so to speak, if he agreed to all the conditions."

"A job?"

"To do the interfering they couldn't do. To go where something was about to go sour and straighten it out for people who deserved it. They'd give him the knowledge he needed and a little . . . help to nudge things in the right direction."

His mouth twisted wryly. "Well, this guy, he figured he was dead anyway, so he said yes. What did it matter, since it was only a hallucination anyway? Except it wasn't."

"Michael—"

"I know it sounds crazy. But that guy, the next thing he knew, he was outside. In the sun. Breathing." He drew another gulp of air. "He spent a week, in their time, learning the rules."

"Their time?"

"Yeah. Their time is a lot different. A month here is about a day to them."

Her eyes narrowed, but she let it pass. "The rules?"

He smiled wryly, ticking them off like a child reciting a lesson. "No violence. No lying, except by omission. No interference in anything that doesn't have a direct bearing on the job you're sent to do. And above all, no one finds out who—or what—you are."

He could see the doubt in her eyes, warring with the memory of the incontrovertible evidence she had seen last night.

"I know, Alex. I didn't believe it, either, at first."

"You . . . were the man in that mine?"

He nodded.

"Michael . . . when was that?"

Here it came, he thought. She would be sure he was crazy now. "September twenty-ninth."

Something flared in her eyes as her dilemma deepened. "What year, Michael?" she asked softly.

"I think you already know that."

Her eyes fell to the golden tags that lay on his chest. "But that was over a hundred years ago."

"I told you their time was different. That was part of what they gave me."

"Part?"

"They gave me vision. Second sight, if you like. The power of will, and the ability to extend it to others, to plant ideas, to make things happen. The power to read people, even past the masks they wear. And, when necessary, some powers I can't quite explain."

Alex paled. "You mean like...warning people from a mile away?"

Slowly, wondering if she was going to be able to accept this, he nodded.

"I...I heard you," she said shakily. "I would have ridden right over that drop. I thought later I'd been hearing things, but—"

"You weren't."

She just sat there, and he could see her trying to absorb it all. At last she met his eyes. "That first day, when you came here..."

"I was due for a vacation. Overdue. They owed it to me, but they dropped me here instead."

"Why?" This was crazy. *She* was crazy, for even listening.

"Because you asked for help."

She sat up straight. "I what?"

"Help not to give up the fight for the refuge."

"I..." She faltered, remembering the day that weary plea had escaped her battered heart. Her head was reeling, her common sense screaming that this was all insane, but there was too much that she couldn't explain away.

"All the things you fixed...the wood that shouldn't have been usable...the shingles you found...my truck...and you weren't hurt in the fire, when you should have been dead...oh, God, and Mark..."

"Yes. They gave me that, too."

Her eyes fell on the tags once more. "Those are..."

"My connection with them."

"Oh, Michael."

"I'm sorry, Alex. None of this was supposed to happen."

"But you said they helped you control things...." Lord, when had she started to believe all this craziness?

"They blew it," he said flatly.

She stared at him.

"In all those years, I've never gotten...personally involved. It was part of the deal. They weren't...human, but they understood human nature. That it would eventually kill a man to come to...care about the people he was helping, and yet always have to leave them behind. To have them all die, eventually, while he went on. They took care of that. I don't know how they numbed that capacity to feel, but they did. I've never felt any personal attachment, ever. Until you."

Alex was gaping at him now.

"I don't know what happened. It wasn't supposed to. It never has." He glanced at the tags. "I don't think they know, either. It really shook them up, when I told them."

"Told them...what?"

With the greatest effort of his life, he held her gaze. "That I love you."

Alex gasped, then stifled a tiny cry. The shutters that had blocked her soul from him fell away, and light leaped into the green depths of her eyes. She came out of the chair in a rush, scrambling down beside him on the bed.

"Oh, Michael, I love you, too."

His hands shot up to grip her shoulders, and he held her up and away from him as he stared at her, stunned.

"You...do? I know you thought you did, before, but—"

"Of course I do!"

"But I thought...you said you'd already made up your mind...after last night...."

"Oh, God, Michael, I meant that I'd already made up my mind that I still love you, no matter what the explanation was for what I saw."

"Alex..." His voice was suddenly thick. "I know I'm...different, Alex, and you looked at me like I was... Your eyes were so...cold."

"Because I didn't understand. I thought you...didn't trust me, because you hadn't told me. Oh, I don't mean I understand now—it all sounds so crazy—but all that matters is that I love you."

She turned her head to kiss the fingers of the hands that held her. He shivered.

"Alex, stop. You *don't* understand. That's why I had to...stop last night. When you're safe, when my job is done here, I—"

"You'll leave."

"I have to. It's one of the rules."

"But you said...they owe you a vacation." She lowered her eyes to the tags, caught between her breasts as she lay on his chest. "Don't you get to choose where you take it?"

"Alex," he breathed. "Oh, God, Alex, don't you get it? Even if I could stay for a while, I'd still have to leave. I can't promise you the future you deserve. And I can't just...make love to you, knowing that."

"*You* don't understand, Michael. I'd rather have one day with you, if that's all I'm allowed, than the rest of my life with anyone else." She lifted one slender hand to brush back his tousled hair. "Besides," she said with the barest flicker of a grin, "how could a girl resist a man who's waited for her for a hundred years?"

He gaped at her, stunned. Then, welling up from so deep inside him that she could feel it before she heard it, he laughed. Long and deep and joyous, it washed over her like warm, soft rain, soothing away all the ache and hurt. He moved to cup her face in his hands.

"A hundred years," he said solemnly, "could make a guy a little rusty."

She blushed. "I didn't notice a problem last night."

"Now that you mention it," he said, sky blue eyes sparkling, "neither did I. There's a lot to be said for instinct, I guess."

"Too much."

"What?"

"Too much to be said. Please don't."

Again he laughed, and she thought that despite all the times she's seen his eyes gleam with that uncanny glow, she'd never seen them alight like this.

"Just what would you suggest I do instead?"

She reached down and lifted the golden tags. "Get rid of our audience."

Still chuckling, he tugged them off, but as he tossed them on the nightstand once more, Alex looked uneasy.

"Will they . . . will you get in trouble?"

"They never thought it would happen, so they never gave me any rules about this. They never counted on you, Alexandra."

She didn't even mind the name, not the way he said it, drawn out as if it were something regal. He pulled her down to him, his mouth seeking hers. She gave a glad little cry and met him, lips soft and warm, the nerves in her scalp tingling as his strong fingers threaded through her hair. His heat flooded her as his tongue invaded her mouth, stroking the ridge of her teeth, probing into every secret place.

Her own tongue sought his, teasing, dancing over the hot, rough velvet. He groaned low in his throat at her eager responsiveness and crushed her lips as he deepened the kiss.

He shoved the pillows aside, keeping her carefully atop him. He lifted himself slightly, savoring the slight weight of her. She went slack, letting herself press downward as if she'd read his need and echoed it.

"Lex," he murmured, trailing his mouth down the side of her throat. She threw her head back, baring the slender arc for his lips. The movement pressed her against him through the cloth of her robe. With a low, throttled sound he slid his hands down from her shoulders to cup the outer curves of her breasts.

She gave a muffled cry, and in an instinctive response, she braced her hands on his chest and raised herself over him. The movement freed her breasts, and the sight of them swaying beneath the pale green robe as she hovered there sent a blast of undeniable need through him. He slipped the worn cloth from her shoulders, then down her arms, baring the full, tempting curves, each tipped with a perfect pink crest.

Alex moaned, feeling her already tingling nipples contract as he looked at her. Michael echoed that groan as he saw the pink deepen to rose and the soft flesh tighten and peak under just his gaze. He moved his hands to cup the feminine softness, lifting the sweet weight, heat cascading through him at the feel of her filling his hands, at the sight of those taut nipples going rigid at the first touch of his hands on her flesh. A pulsing, throbbing heat settled somewhere low and deep inside him, hardening him in a single, fierce rush.

Those two beckoning crests were a temptation too great for him to resist, and he lifted his head to flick his tongue over them, savoring Alex's tiny cry as she arched toward him, letting her head loll back as she closed her eyes. The movement pressed her hips hard against his, her stomach against his eager, demanding flesh.

It might have been a long time, and that time buried in what primal memory they had let him keep, but his body remembered perfectly, and it was hot and hard and aching. He looked up at her, at the slender curve of her throat, the quivering of her breasts as she thrust them toward him, and at her glistening nipples, wet from his mouth.

He gave a hoarse groan as his head shot upward, capturing and tugging at one of the begging peaks with his lips. He suckled softly, then deeply, feeling Alex's response in the exclamation that broke from her on a breathless gasp, in the eager bowing of her body to give him more of the honeyed sweetness of her breasts, and the way her fingers dug into the muscles of his chest. His aching flesh pressed against her, trapped in a sweet caress between them. Convulsively his hips jerked as he moved to her other breast, drawing the taut nipple deeply into his mouth and flicking it with his tongue.

"Michael," she gasped. "Oh, Michael!"

"I know, Lexie, I know," he muttered.

He was on fire, sizzling with the heat that erupted anew with every touch, with every sliding of skin over skin, with every eager shiver of response that he drew from her. He tugged at the tangled robe, and with a quick little shake of her shoulders, she helped him. It slid to the floor, forgotten. He tugged off his briefs, then nudged her gently to one side as he kicked the covers away, needing the feel of her naked body against his with an urgency that stunned him.

Alex cried out in shocked pleasure as he rolled her beneath him, startled by how good it felt to have his weight bearing down on her. She could feel the column of aroused male flesh hard against her own softness, starting a hollow ache she'd never known before in some deep, private place inside her.

He was so hot and strong and solid, and her body ached to be even closer. Her arms went around him, her hands stroking over the muscles of his back, loving the feel of his skin, smooth and sleek as it slid over rock-hard muscle. She remembered the day they'd built the barn, remembered the way she'd felt as she'd watched him move, watched the flex and play of the muscles in his back, chest, and belly. And now that beautiful body, naked and fully aroused, was in her arms, setting her on fire in a way she'd never dreamed of. She tried, in broken little phrases, to tell him.

"No, Alex. It's you who's beautiful." His mouth lingered over one breast, and she felt the erotic brush of his breath as he spoke. "You know that now, don't you?"

"I know you make me feel beautiful," she whispered, unable to stop herself from arching her back again, thrusting her breast to him until the aching, beseeching nipple brushed his lips.

"You are," he murmured, letting the vibration of his voice tickle the tingling peak. "Inside and out, Alex." Then he took her nipple fiercely, making her cry out with the sudden burst of sweet, rippling sensation.

She felt his knee slide between hers, urging her legs apart. She opened for him eagerly, shuddering with pleasure as he slipped between her parted thighs. Her hands slid down his back to cup the tightly muscled curve of his buttocks, trying to draw him closer. She did it without thinking, only knowing that she couldn't bear this aching emptiness inside any longer, and only he could end it. Only he could ease the ache; only he could fill the hollowness inside her with the sweet, hot gift of himself.

"Alex," Michael said thickly, "Alex, are you sure?"

"Yes," she gasped, twisting sinuously beneath him. "I need you, Michael."

He groaned, burying his face in the soft curve of her neck and shoulder. "I want...I don't know how slow I can go—"

"It's all right," she whispered. "I know it will hurt at first—"

"Hurt?" He lifted his head to stare down into her eyes. "Alex you mean you've never...?" He closed his eyes as the truth that should have been obvious hit him. "Of course you haven't," he said, his voice rough. "After what that bastard did to you..."

"Michael, no. It doesn't matter. It has nothing to do with this, with us."

"No. No, it doesn't."

He lowered his head to kiss her lips softly. A virgin. Lord, what now? He didn't want to hurt her; she'd been hurt so much already. A thought came to him, and he paused, considering. He didn't like the idea, didn't want it, but if it would save her pain. . . .

"Alex? I can . . . make it not hurt."

It took a moment for his meaning to penetrate the hot haze of pleasure that surrounded her. Her answer came quickly, unhesitantly.

"No, Michael," she whispered. "I don't want that between us. We're together here and now. It's real, and I don't want anything but that reality. Just you and me."

It was as if she'd reached into his soul and pulled out the very essence of his reluctance, and he shivered a little as he hugged her fiercely. He began to kiss her, soft little suckling kisses that left a line of fire up and down her body, down the line of her shoulder, over the full rise of her breasts, lingering at the throbbing nipples, down over the concave curve of her stomach, over the point of her hip to the soft flesh of her thigh.

When he lifted her to his mouth, parting the soft auburn curls with his tongue, Alex cried out as the intimate kiss sent flaring, crackling sparks through her in a fountain of golden heat. He tortured her with quick, darting caresses, until she was bucking with wild abandon.

At the moment when she cried out to him that she couldn't bear any more, he moved over her, his eager demanding flesh seeking the heat he'd created in her with all the urgency he'd fought so hard to suppress.

A low, harsh rasp of sound broke from him at the first touch of her slick heat as her body yielded to his. She was rippling in his arms, tiny little cries rising from her, her hands raking over his back. He tried to go slow, every muscle in his body standing out with the strain. Then she lifted her hips, taking him deeper, until he could feel the resistance of that fragile barrier.

"Please, Michael," she gasped.

The breathy little plea sent him careering out of control, and with one convulsive jerk of his hips, he thrust forward, deep and home.

Alex gave one small cry of pain, but it was forgotten as soon as it left her lips, lost in the wonder of the feel of him deep and full inside her. She felt him shudder, heard her name escape him in a voice so thick and husky with pleasure it was barely recognizable, felt the throbbing of that swollen male flesh that had so sweetly invaded her body. He had filled her beyond all expectation, erasing that hollowness as if it had never been, stretching her to an exquisite tightness.

Then, with a ragged groan, he began to move. He began with long, slow strokes, measuring his rigid length in her again and again. Then she began to move with him, lifting her hips to meet his thrusts, and he exploded into frantic action. Alex went flying with him, soaring, her only connection to the earth that had always held her was the sound of her name in that deep, husky voice.

"Alex," he gasped, his hands gripping her shoulders as he drove deep into her again. "I . . . can't . . . wait. . . ."

Her nails dug into his back, and she nipped lightly at his shoulder with a boldness that would have startled her had she been able to feel anything except her body racing toward an explosion she couldn't even imagine. And then she was there, every part of her erupting into a spray of heat and fire and spinning light. She cried out his name, a touch of fear in her voice as she lost her hold on the earth. But he was there with her, holding her so very tightly, so very sweetly, her name breaking from him in a choking shout as he exploded within her, pouring all the yearnings of years into her sweet, hot depths.

"Alex?" he murmured much later, as he lay with her cradled in his arms, their legs still entwined.

"Mmm?"

"Those hundred years? This was worth every minute."

She giggled, a low, carefree sound that sent a ripple of delight up his spine. "I'm afraid I can only claim twenty-six years of waiting, but I'm very glad I did."

"So am I," he whispered. "Did I hurt you very much?"

"I don't remember," she said, snuggling closer.

He smiled, nuzzling her hair with his lips. "I'm glad."

After a while she said softly, "Michael?"

"Hmm?"

"Why did they pick you?"

He chuckled. "I'd like to say that it was because I was such a great guy, but that ain't it. I just happened to meet their qualifications."

"What do you mean?"

He shrugged. "I was alone, basically. Not that it would have made any difference to anyone I might have left behind, since I would have died anyway, but it would have been harder on me if there had been someone I'd left, someone that I would have had to walk away from and never see again...."

He faltered, knowing that that was exactly the position he was in now.

Alex read him immediately. "Not now. We won't think about it now."

She pressed a kiss on his cheek, then let her head settle back onto his shoulder. Her arm, stretched across his chest, tightened for a moment in a fierce hug. Then she went on as if the painful subject had never been mentioned.

"What I really meant was, why did they send you here? There are ... more of you, aren't there?"

"A few." He reached up and tweaked her pert nose. "They sent me because they knew I'm a sucker for big green eyes and sassy noses."

"Michael," she said with a mock sternness belied by the twinkle of pleasure in her eyes.

"They sent me," he said with sudden seriousness, "because they knew that once I met you, I'd forget about how mad I was that they'd reneged on their promise that I'd get a break."

"Why? Why would you forget?"

"Because they've infected me, I suppose. I can't stand the thought of injustice, especially when it's against innocence and goodness and honesty and integrity. And you're all of that, Alexandra."

She blushed. "Michael, no, I just—"

"You are, Alex. Take it from an expert."

She had to accept it; he wouldn't listen to any protest. She settled down beside him with a sigh of contentment. She had known it would be sweet, but she had never dreamed it would be so all-consuming. She'd never known anything could be.

She lay there for a long time, savoring the feel of his muscled shoulder beneath her cheek, the steady beat of his heart beneath her hand splayed on his chest, the feel of his hair-roughened thigh between hers. Then, tentatively, she began to explore, her hands moving slowly, then more boldly when he didn't protest.

Her hand slid over the muscled wall of his chest. She felt him jerk sharply, heard his quick intake of breath when her fingers found one of his flat, male nipples. Experimentally she let her hand drift to the other brown nub of flesh, this time feeling a spurt of heat shoot through her own body at his response to her touch.

Her hand slid down over his belly, feeling the deep muscles there ripple beneath her touch. The tiny spark flickered and caught; how potent it was, she thought in wonder, to be wanted in return. How powerful a feeling, to know that she could do this to him.

As if of its own volition, her hand moved downward, then paused as her fingertips reached the thicket of dark, curly hair at the base of his belly. Shyness suddenly swept over her, and she began to pull back. Then his hand was there, over hers, holding it there.

"Anything you want, Alex," he whispered thickly.

Color flooded her cheeks, but the magnet was irresistible, and her fingers crept down to touch that male flesh that was already fiercely responding to her caresses. It was slower this time, but no less sweet, and, in the end, no less urgent, just as the explosion was no less shattering.

Michael was loath to disrupt the sweet silence that followed, but he knew it was time. Still, he couldn't quite stifle a sigh.

"What, love?" she asked softly.

Reflexively his arms tightened around her at the sweetness of the word. But still he couldn't beat back the hovering cloud of things yet to be done, and at last he spoke heavily. "We have to call the sheriff."

She lifted her head to look at him. "Can we? I mean, we can't exactly explain what happened last night."

"They don't need the details. But Mark was shot, and the guy who did it is still out walking around."

She sighed in turn. "I know. But they won't be able to find anything. Matt and Steve went over that hill with a fine-toothed comb. There wasn't a trace."

"I know."

"He's long gone, whoever it was."

"Long, but not far."

Her eyes widened. "Michael? Why did you say it like that? Like you . . . knew?"

His eyes met hers then.

"Because I do," he said softly.

# Ten

―――――

"**W**hy did you wait so long?" Walt asked with an air of mild exasperation.

"We were too worried about Mark," Alex said, and left it at that.

They'd given the young deputy the basics, including the phone calls, but no more.

"You're sure you don't know who it is?" he asked Alex.

Her eyes flicked to Michael. He said nothing, so she answered carefully, "*I* don't have any idea. Except that it has to be the caller."

"We can't prove that," Walt said warningly.

"But he said someone would get hurt—"

"I know, Alex," Walt said. "And you're probably right. I just don't know how we'll prove it. *If* we ever find him."

Alex opened her mouth to speak, then shut it again. She couldn't doubt Michael when he'd said he knew who it was. She remembered too clearly that moment in the woods when she had sensed the wave of realization that had swept him. But he'd told her gently that he couldn't tell her who it was.

"It might affect what happens, Alex. You might act differently around the wrong person. He has to believe no one knows, that you're still scared, or he might run."

She'd laughed a little ruefully. "I *am* still scared."

"Don't be. Nothing will happen to you."

"Like nothing happened to Mark?"

"That was a promise my bosses didn't keep. This one is from me."

An icy determination unlike anything she'd ever seen glowed in the sky blue eyes, and she knew he meant exactly what he said. He would go to any lengths to protect her. It was a new, strange feeling to Alex, and she treasured it even as she wondered at it.

She was yanked back to the present by Michael's unexpected words.

"Where were the animals found?"

Walt gaped at Michael, startled by his seeming non sequitur. "What?"

"The animals that were killed. Where were they found?"

"Three or four different places," Walt said, clearly puzzled. "One on the road near the Morgan place, one out in back of the feed store in town, one down by the river, near the swimming hole—"

"All places where they'd be found almost immediately."

"Well . . ."

"And all in unusual places for livestock to be found."

"I suppose so, but—"

"Was there blood?"

Walt gaped again. "What?"

"Where they were found."

"Well, no, now that you mention it. Not like you'd expect, anyway. But they could have been wounded and just wandered that far. Look, what has that got to do with—"

"It wasn't Cougar," Alex said suddenly.

"Sure, Alex," Walt said soothingly. "I don't think anyone believes that anymore, no matter what Henry says. Not after seeing the way he was with Billy Peterson. Besides, you said you've kept him locked up."

"What if it wasn't an animal at all?" Michael asked.

Walt wheeled around to stare at Michael again. "What?" he said for the third time.

"What if it was someone who wanted everyone to think it was Cougar? To cause more trouble for Alex and the refuge."

"You mean . . . the caller?"

"And the shooter."

"But—"

"It would explain it, wouldn't it? If the animals were killed in one place, then moved to another? It wouldn't take much to make the wounds look ragged, like an animal bite. Especially if he thought no one would look too closely."

After a long moment Walt nodded. "I suppose. But we're back to who again, aren't we? And up until recently, I can think of a dozen people who might have had an interest in shutting this place down."

"We only need one."

Walt looked thoughtful. "Maybe I should talk to Henry," he began.

Michael glanced at Alex, glad to see that no haunting memories shadowed the green eyes at the mention of the name. He had done that, at least, he thought, exorcised that awful demon she'd buried so deep. He turned back to Walt.

"You're a good cop, Walt. And smart enough to look beyond the obvious."

Now that she knew, Alex could almost see it happening. She saw that incredible gleam growing in the clear blue eyes, saw the slightly dazed look come over Walt's face. For several long, silent moments it went on, until at last Michael spoke again, quietly.

"You'll find him, Walt. Just go with your instinct."

"Uh ... yeah." Walt shook his head, looking a little like a wide-eyed owl waking up after a day's sleep. "Sure. I'd better get started."

When he was gone, Alex looked at Michael curiously. "Couldn't you just ... tell him?"

"I could. But it's better if he finds it himself. He'll believe it more if he has to work at it a little."

"But you ... told him where to start, didn't you?"

He didn't deny it. "I gave him a nudge in the right direction."

"You seem to do a lot of that."

He shrugged. "Most people want to go in the right direction. Sometimes they just need a little help finding it." He grimaced. "So do I sometimes. I had the wrong guy for a while, because I had something personal against him. But Walt will have the right one, soon."

Alex's eyes went to the golden tags he'd put back on this morning when Walt had arrived, then back to his face.

"You've seen such wonders, haven't you, Michael?" she said in a hushed tone. "I wish—" She stopped, dropping her gaze.

"What, Alex?"

"Nothing."

"Tell me."

Her head came up. "I wish we...had time. I'd like to hear about things you've seen."

"Time." It came out flatly, sourly. "Time," he repeated. "We're going to get that time, Alex." He stopped, looking at her steadily. "If you're sure you want it. But it might make it worse, in the end." His voice dropped, pained. "And it has to end, Alex. I can't quit."

He hated saying it, but he couldn't let her hope, not when it was impossible. She met his gaze unflinchingly.

"I know that. And I told you, I'd rather have whatever time they allow me with you than all the time I have left with someone else. I love you, Michael."

He pulled her into his arms. "Oh, God, Alex. I love you, too." He held her for a long moment before he gripped her shoulders and looked down into her face. "I guess I'd better talk to the bosses."

"Now?"

He nodded. She stepped back, her eyes fastened on the gold tags a little warily.

"If they're mad, tell them it's their own fault."

He smiled. "I will." He studied her for a moment. "Will you come with me?"

"Can I?"

For answer he took her hand, then began to walk toward the quiet little clearing he'd come to use as a refuge of his own.

"Michael?"

"What?"

"What if they had kept you from . . . feeling anything for me? Do you think I would have still—" She broke off, then answered her own question. "Of course I would have. How could I not love you?"

His hand tightened around hers. "Thank you. But I think it . . . I don't know. It's like there's been some kind of barrier, all these years, that everyone could sense even if they didn't understand it. It kept them all away. Until you found a way through it." He grinned at her. "You were just too much for them, Alexandra Logan."

They reached the small clearing and sat down on the cool grass. He gave her a quick look of reassurance, and then his hand went to the tags.

*Michael! Are you all right? We've been very concerned.*
Fine.
*You're certain? We felt the drain. We were afraid we'd lost you.*
I'm fine. Thank you.
*Thank you? For what?*
For the help. Mark is going to be okay.

*Good. Michael, are you sure you're all right? You sound very odd.*

Yes, I am. But I'm very tired.

*We realize that, Michael. And we realize that we've been unfair with you. We've put you under too much strain. It's only natural that you should imagine a fondness for—*

It's not a "fondness," and I'm not imagining it.

*I understand how strong these . . . urges are in humans. Perhaps we underestimated the power of such a strong attraction. But it can be fixed.*

This is not something you can "fix." I don't know what went wrong—or right—but I love her.

*Michael, you know that's impossible.*

It's true, nevertheless.

*But we made certain that something like this would never happen. I—*

Goofed. And she says to tell you it's all your own fault.

A silence, stunned this time; Michael wasn't sure how he could tell, but he knew. He answered the unspoken question wryly.

Yes, I broke that rule, too. She saw me with Mark. She had to know. And it won't matter, later.

That, Michael thought with amazement, was a sigh. First they drop that damn royal "we," and now they're sighing.

*I suppose you're right.* Then, indignantly, *Did she really say that?*

Yes.

A pause. *She believed you, then.*

Yes.

*Unusual.*

So is she.

*Yes. Hmm. Well, we could bring you back here for some readjustment, I suppose. Perhaps that's all that's wrong.*

No. It's not a matter of adjustment.

*But for all of these years of yours—*

It worked. But it only worked for one reason.

*What?*

Because I hadn't met Alex.

A pause.

You said she was as special as she seemed. It was an understatement. Don't blame me if I see it, too.

*We don't blame you, Michael. We just don't quite know what to do.*

I'll tell you what you're going to do.

*I beg your pardon?*

You're going to give me that vacation you owe me.

*Well of course we are. As soon as you're done. It will be soon, won't it?*

Very.

*Good. Now, where would you like to go?*

Nowhere.

*But you just said . . .*

I'm staying here.

Another pause. *You know we can't allow that.*

Then I quit.

*You can't do that, either.*

Watch me.

*You know what that means, Michael.*

Yes.

*It means that much to you? You'd go back to that awful hole in the ground, knowing the result?*

I'd be just as dead if I walked away from her now.

*You'd be giving yourself just that many more memories to live with later. Is it worth that price to you?*

It's worth any price.

They didn't answer. He clutched the tags tighter, waiting. Still nothing. He knew he was bargaining with his life, but he also knew that they wouldn't pull him before his job was done. No matter what their decision, he would have that much time. After that, if they made him leave, it wouldn't matter. Nothing would. He waited.

Still nothing. A sudden rush of uncharacteristic anger filled him. He'd done everything they asked, all this time. He'd been all over the world for years on end. He'd seen more tragedies than anyone should ever have to look upon. And never once, until now, had he even asked for a break, let alone anything for himself.

He scrambled to his feet, tearing the tags over his head. He let the full force of his temper go through, not caring anymore. He leaned back, cocked his arm and, with all his strength, flung the golden tags up and away from him.

They twirled in midair, soaring up out of the shadows of the trees and into the sun, catching the light in golden glints. And then, in a sudden flare of brilliant golden sparks, they disappeared.

Michael closed his eyes as he sank back to the grass; his strength had drained away the minute the tags had been claimed by their true owners. So this was it, he thought, his head spinning as he gasped for air. He'd been wrong. They'd decided to pull him anyway. When he opened his eyes, if he lasted that long, he'd be back in the dark, his lungs on fire as he tried to eke out a last few seconds of life.

He shuddered, but he made himself do it. And opened his eyes to the dappled sun and Alex's face. Stunned, he sat up.

"I'm still here," he whispered. "I thought they'd put me back."

"Back?"

Alex barely managed to get it out; believing what he'd told her and seeing the incontrovertible proof of it with her own eyes were two different things, she discovered.

"To the mine. I thought . . . That's what was supposed to happen. If I quit."

She looked at him, wide-eyed. When he'd told her he couldn't quit, she hadn't realized that the reason was that it would cost him his life. Alex paled.

"They wouldn't! Not after all you've done!"

He was a little steadier now. "It was one of the conditions, Alex. If I quit, they had to put me back. It didn't seem too bad at the time, compared to the alternative."

"You did that, risked that . . . to stay with me?"

"I had no choice," he said simply. "I love you. I didn't know what they'd do, but I had to try."

"But what if they—"

"I know." He pulled her into his arms as he let out a sigh. "Whatever it is they've done, all this time, it's worked well up to now. It never mattered to me before, being alone. Not feeling any real emotion for anyone. Not needing anyone. Not loving anyone. It made sense. It was the only way it could work. But now . . ."

"What will they do?"

He laughed wryly. "You mean now that you've come along and blown all their calculations to bits? I don't know. They still can't figure out what happened."

"But . . ." She hugged him tightly, even as a shudder went through her at the idea of him, even as a bluff, thinking of going back to that death trap. "You're still here."

"Yes." He went suddenly tense, cocking his head. Then his eyes fluttered closed as he swallowed tightly.

"Michael?"

When he opened his eyes, it was to give her a tenderly joyous look. "We've got a month," he whispered.

Her eyes widened. "Oh, Michael," she breathed as she hugged him fiercely again.

He held her close, pressing his lips against her hair. "It's not forever, Alex. I wish it could be."

"Any time at all is more of a gift than I ever expected in my life," she said softly.

She meant it, and in the days that followed she tried to live it. It took one of the greatest efforts of her life, but Alex put the shadow hovering over them out of her mind. She was determined to make the most of these precious days, determined to store up as many sweet, honeyed memories as she could for the long, lonely time to come.

The others seemed to blithely accept the changes in her, the way she bloomed before their eyes. They never commented on the fact that Michael had changed his sleeping quarters, or that every time anyone found them together, they were in each other's arms. And they silently took over many of her chores, giving her more free time than she'd ever had.

Mark came home from the clinic, weak but healing rapidly. He claimed to remember nothing that had happened after he'd been shot, but Alex had seen something flicker in his eyes when he shook Michael's hand.

"Knew you were special," was all he said.

Every day seemed more beautiful than the last, and Alex hummed happily as she groomed Cricket, brushing his black-and-white coat until it gleamed like the wet hide of a killer whale. They had taken to riding double on the big stallion whenever they had a free moment, savoring the deep pine scents and crisp air of her beloved Oregon countryside.

Michael had laughed at first, telling her that his only riding experience was longer ago than he cared to remember. But he'd grown to love it as much as she did, and this day was no different.

"Want to drive?" she asked as she led the big horse outside.

"No thanks," he said with a wicked grin. "I like having my hands free."

Alex blushed furiously and took a teasing swipe at him with the reins. He laughed and gave her a leg up onto the horse's broad back. He leapt up behind her and settled into his accustomed spot, with her nestled closely between his strong thighs. His arms came around her, locking beneath her breasts and pulling her even tighter against him.

Alex felt the warmth that was so familiar to her now begin to radiate through her body from beneath his hands. Every day it seemed that it took less time for that aching need to build in her; sometimes it took only a look from him to bring it to life, full-grown and demanding.

She let out a tiny sigh and heard Michael chuckle behind her. He let his hands slip downward and pulled her hips back

against him, letting her feel the instant effect her closeness
had on him.

"Wonder how far we'll get this time?" he asked her
huskily as he leaned around to nibble her ear.

The sound she made was half laugh, half gasp. So many
times their rides had come to an abrupt end when the desire
that seemed to be always simmering just under the surface
came to a boil so suddenly and fiercely that it couldn't be
ignored.

Alex blushed as she thought of the unlikely places they'd
made love: a clearing near the bank of the river, on a bed of
pine needles up the hill near home, and once, when the need
had grown too great too quickly, in the hayloft over Cricket's stall. The need for quiet then had somehow added to
their fervency, as if the feelings they couldn't vent with their
voices were transferred to their bodies, making their gasping, silent climax even more shattering.

Michael's thoughts were apparently going along the same
lines, for his hands became more urgent as they moved over
her, pressing against the flat of her stomach, then rising to
cup and lift her breasts.

When they were out of sight of the farm, up in the trees
on the hill, Alex dropped the reins and let Cricket go where
he wanted. She lifted her hands back over her shoulders to
lock behind Michael's neck and draw him down to her. The
movement arched her back, moving her breasts against his
hands. He groaned low in his throat, and his fingers fum-
bled with the buttons of her shirt.

Alex felt the insistent pressure of his aroused flesh against
the curve of her buttocks and reflexively moved against him.
Then she could feel nothing but hot, pulsing pleasure as he
freed her breasts for his hands.

They made it as far as a quiet, shaded clearing near where
they had found Mark before they tumbled from Cricket's
back to the grassy carpet. They tugged at each other's
clothes, kissing and caressing every inch of skin they ex-
posed, until at last they could wait no longer.

Michael rolled to his back and pulled Alex over him. She had lost the last of her shyness days ago and straddled him eagerly, lowering herself to take him in with a glad cry. He reached up to caress her taut nipples as she rocked on him, the tiny sounds of pleasure she made blending with his low murmuring of her name.

She felt it begin, that rising, swirling tide, and her slow pace became urgent. Michael felt the change, and his body responded with the swiftness he'd come to expect with her. Soon he was moving her, arching up into her with all his strength, loving the cries that broke from her and the way her fingers curled desperately into his shoulders as she rode him so sweetly. The first rippling contractions of her body around his were his undoing, and he felt himself erupt inside her in wave after wave of hot, fierce pleasure.

"Alex . . . Lex . . . Lexieee . . ."

He shuddered as she collapsed, trembling, atop him, his name coming from her on a long, shivery breath.

"God, I love you," he said fervently when he could speak again. "All these years, I've watched people . . . I knew that it worked. Love, I mean. I knew how it worked, what it did to people . . . but I never knew how it felt. That it could be so hot, so sweet."

For a time, just for a while, Alex let herself think that it would never end. That they could go on like this forever, that the beautiful dream would never stop. Then, when three weeks of their precious month had gone, the outside world came crashing back in with shocking force.

They came back from a ride to find Walt's unit parked in front of the house. Walt was leaning against the fender, but he straightened as soon as he saw them coming. Alex could feel his eyes going over them speculatively. By the time she slid off Cricket's back in front of him, the young deputy wore the expression of a man who had just reached an unexpected conclusion and was not too happy about it. But his voice was amiable enough.

"We got him, Alex."

Alex let out a long breath. "Thank God." Then, after a moment, apprehensively, "Was it Henry?"

"No."

Alex let out a sigh of relief. She hadn't liked the idea of having to tell the world why Henry had disliked her enough to do all this.

"I thought it was, at first," Walt said, "but then I thought maybe I just didn't like the guy."

Alex gave a little start as a memory clicked into place. She turned to stare at Michael. "I had the wrong guy for a while," he'd said, "because I had something personal against him." Now she understood; it was Henry he'd been talking about, and the something personal was what he'd done to her so long ago.

"Anyway," Walt went on, drawing her attention once more, "something kept nagging at me to check some other things out." He glanced at Michael with a look that was curiously puzzled. "That instinct you mentioned, I guess."

Michael shrugged. "I knew you had it."

"Well," Walt said, pleased with himself, "you must be right. Only thing I can think of that made me pull Ray over."

"Ray?" Alex asked. Walt nodded.

"Yep. Ray Claridge. I found the knife he used on the animals, blood in the back of his truck . . . and a pistol under the seat."

"A gun?" Alex's breath caught. "Mark?"

Walt nodded again. "Haven't got the ballistics back yet, but it's the same caliber. Besides, Ray copped out when he realized I'd found the gun and could match it with the bullet Doc took out of Mark. He admitted the phone calls, too."

"But . . . why?" Alex stared at the deputy. "He's never been one of the complainers. He never acted like he cared one way or the other if we were here."

"He was afraid that if the town came to accept you, they might look at him and start remembering."

"Remembering?"

Walt looked uncomfortable. "He...I guess you were too young at the time..."

"Walt, what are you talking about? Why on earth would Ray want to hurt us?"

Michael put his hands on her shoulders comfortingly. "Do you remember him?" he asked.

"Not really. I remember he and my brother never got along. Ray was always trying to bad-mouth Andrew behind his back. But he left town when I was young to take a job up north. He's only been back a few years."

"He didn't leave for a job," Walt said.

"He didn't?" She turned away from Michael to look at Walt. "But his father said he was—"

"He left because he'd been drafted."

Alex's eyes widened. Michael nodded.

"He went to Canada. He came back under the amnesty program," Walt went on.

"But—"

"He was afraid that if the town started to see the men at the refuge as the brave men they are, they might change their minds about accepting what he had done. He'd always insisted it was because he objected to the war, but I think he knew not very many believed that. Besides, he'd always hated your brother. And Gary Swan," Walt finished.

"But why?"

Michael gave her a gentle smile. "Because everyone else liked and admired them. He was jealous of them both when they were alive, and more so after they died. Then Henry told him, one night when they'd been out drinking, what he'd done to you."

Alex flushed and glanced at Walt. He'd been staring in surprise at Michael, but when he looked up, he quickly averted his eyes. She knew then that he knew, and embarrassment filled her. But Michael took her hand and it faded away. He went on softly.

"Ray never had the nerve to fight face-to-face, so he concocted this plan to scare you off and get Henry blamed for it. And Henry only helped by mouthing off about Cougar. Not only did Ray hope it would close down the refuge, it was his way of getting back at Andrew. And Gary, too, in a way, because he loved both you and Andrew so much. He figured you were vulnerable, and he had a hold on Henry because of what he knew. But it got out of hand when Mark found him skulking around the farm, and Ray shot him."

Michael stopped as he realized Walt was gaping at him, his surprise turned to shock.

"How did you find all that out? I only figured it all out yesterday."

"I . . . just put two and two together."

"Maybe you should be a cop."

"No thanks. I don't have the fortitude." He held out a hand. "Nice work, Walt," he said evenly, holding Walt's gaze unflinchingly.

"Er, yeah." An odd expression came over Walt's face as he shook Michael's hand. Then his mouth twisted wryly. "I'm still not sure how it happened, though. I just seemed to keep heading in that direction."

"A good cop has good instincts, Walt. You just followed them."

Diverted, Walt muttered a thank you.

Only when he'd gone did the significance of the morning's revelations hit Alex. They were walking toward the barn when she stopped dead, staring up at him.

"It's . . . done now, isn't it? Your job here?"

He took a long, slow breath and nodded.

She cringed inwardly, pain flaring in her eyes. Michael reached for her and she clung to him, fighting tears.

"We still have a week," she said fiercely. "They promised."

"I know, love. We still have a week."

Alex seemed determined to cram as much as she could into that precious time. They rarely slept. They talked, walked for hours, rode for hours more, and made sweet lingering love until they were both spent. And one night, driven by the demons of the hovering future, Michael made love to her time after time, until she was quivering, until one shuddering explosion blended into the next and into the next and she collapsed in limp, sated exhaustion in his arms.

When she woke up, it was to the dreaded sight of the golden tags once more around his neck.

"No!" she cried. "No, not yet!"

"Alex," he began, reaching for her. She jerked out of his reach, and, pulling on her clothes as she went, she ran out of the room, out of the house, tears streaming down her face.

He found her in the clearing behind the house, sitting on the small patch of soft grass. Her cheeks were still damp, but the stream of tears had stopped. She looked up as he dropped down beside her.

"I'm sorry, Michael," she said in a tightly controlled voice. "I thought I was prepared, but I wasn't."

He pulled her into his arms. "I know, Lexie-girl, I know. Neither was I."

"You knew, didn't you? Last night?"

"Not really. Sensed it, maybe." He gave a sigh so weary that it frightened her. He flicked the golden tags with one finger. "I should have known I hadn't seen the last of them." She felt him tremble, knew this was as hard for him as it was for her. "I love you, Alex. I'll love you forever."

"You will, won't you?" Her voice caught at the ironic truth of his words. "I love you, Michael. I'll always love you."

"I know."

"You can't . . . ever come back?"

"No. Never."

"Then I'll live on the memories," she whispered. "I . . . they're sweeter than most people's lives."

He went very still. "Alex . . ."

"What, love?"

"There won't . . . be any memories."

She pulled back to look at him. "What do you mean?"

"When I go . . . you'll forget."

"I could never forget, Michael."

"You will. Everyone will. You'll remember what happened, but not my part in it. You won't remember me at all."

"Michael, no!"

"Yes, Alex. It's the way it works. And it's better that way. Really."

Alex stared at him, horrified. "How can you say that?"

He sat up and took her hands, holding them tightly. He wished he hadn't begun this at all; he hadn't meant to. But now that he had, he had to explain. "Listen to me. What we've had is . . . special. Different. You said it yourself. It's sweeter than anything most people ever have in their lives. If they left you with those memories, you'd spend the rest of your life looking for something to match them. It would never happen, Alex, and you'd be alone forever. You weren't meant to be alone."

"No," she moaned. "Please, Michael, no. They're all I'll have of you."

"I can't, Alex. It's not negotiable."

"It will be like we never were," she cried softly. "Like I'd never met you, or you'd never met me—"

His eyes darted away but not swiftly enough. "Michael?"

He wouldn't look at her, and that gave her her answer.

"You'll remember, won't you?" she whispered hoarsely. "Michael?"

Her hand went to his chin to turn him to face her, and she read in his eyes the knowledge of the long years of torture ahead, years of remembering, yet being able to do nothing, of longing yet having to stay away, and, ultimately, of knowing, years from now, of her death and still having to go on endlessly.

*"No!"* she cried out in a voice fiercer, more ringing, than it had been in her own pain. "They can't do this to you! They can't expect you to go through such hell! They can't!"

"Alex—"

"No! If they're these wonderful, kind beings you say they are, they would never do this! There must be a way!"

"A way to what?" he asked gently, his heart aching as he looked at her agonized, tear-stained face.

"To make you forget, too," she said hoarsely, brokenly.

Michael stared at her. "You *want* me to forget you?"

"I can't bear the thought of you hurting like that," she choked out, fighting the sobs that threatened to take over. "I'd rather lose everything, the refuge, my home... I'd rather Ray had gotten me with that gun than to have you hurt like that. There has to be a way they can make you forget."

"Oh, God, Alex," he murmured, pulling her hard and close against him. He'd never felt so humbled as he did now, faced with the power of this woman's love. He rocked her, cradled her, even as his arms shook with his pain and hers.

"What?"

He looked at her as she lifted her head. "What, Alex?"

Her brows furrowed over reddened eyes. "What did you say?"

"I didn't say anything."

"But I heard—" She paled suddenly, putting a hand to her head. "There it is again. It *wasn't* you!" Her head jerked around as she scanned the trees around them frantically.

"Alex—"

"I heard it," she insisted. "It was my name. I—"

Michael swore softly. He grabbed the tags, and the connection was so immediate that he knew he'd been right.

It *was* you. Knock it off, you're scaring her.

*Sorry, Michael. Can you bring her in?*

He couldn't help being suspicious.

Why?

*Please, Michael.*

He sighed. With an effort he withdrew part of his consciousness from the contact and turned it to Alex's wide-eyed face.

"They want to talk to you," he said. "It's up to you."

She recovered quickly. "Good," she snapped, some of her battered spirit returning. "I've got a few words for them."

Michael smothered a smile. This, he thought, should be interesting. "Hold up your hand." She did, and he laced his fingers with hers, the gold tags caught between their palms. "Close your eyes," he urged. "It makes it easier. Just think the words."

*Alex?*

She tried it.

Yes.

*Good. We wanted to—*

I don't care what you want.

A startled pause. *I beg your pardon?*

What I want is for you to live up to your billing. To the faith Michael has in you.

*Live up to. . . ?*

If you were everything he thinks you are, you would never put him through what you know is coming.

*My, she is a little. . . feisty, isn't she?*

Michael chuckled. Don't say you weren't warned.

*Yes. Quite.* Then, to Alex, although she wasn't sure how she knew. *You meant what you said? That you'd rather he forgot you?*

Yes.

*From our observations over time, it's most unusual for a woman to want to be forgotten. Why?*

Because I love him. And I'd rather be forgotten than cause him pain.

*I see.*

A new voice then, and one that made Michael stiffen with surprise. The big boss, he communicated to Alex swiftly.

*You were always exceptional, Michael.*

Were?

Michael "said" it a little shakily; the voice ignored him.

*Your choice of a mate is only further proof of that. She is as extraordinary as you are.*

Michael gulped.

*But then, it would take an extraordinary woman to make a man give up immortality, wouldn't it?*

Alex gasped as Michael gathered his nerve to go on.

Am I?

*So it seems. You've had a grand run, my boy. You've more than earned this, if it is what you want.*

The yes he sent them was resounding, without hesitation or doubt.

*Good luck, then, Michael. To both of you.*

Alex's mind was too stunned to make much sense, but they seemed to understand.

*You've won, my dear. And, may I say, never have I taken more joy in losing a battle. If Michael hadn't chosen you for his own, I would have looked into recruiting you, if the chance ever arose. Goodbye, children.*

The connection was gone, leaving them both dazed by the sudden exit. Then Alex's vision cleared as the tags between their hands began to glow, to shimmer with a golden light. And then they were gone, as if they'd never been.

Slowly Michael flexed his hand, feeling an odd weight, as if the tags were still there. Then he looked, and in his palm rested two plain, gold rings that seemed to shimmer with a strange light. Alex gasped, her eyes flicking around as if there would be some trace of their benefactors.

"A final gift," Michael murmured as he held up the rings. "Will you wear my ring, Alex? Will you marry me?"

"Of course," she whispered, her eyes glistening. "How could I turn down the man who literally gave up immortality for me?"

And as they joined together in that little clearing, somewhere far away a pleased laugh floated on the wind.

\*     \*     \*     \*     \*

# FOUR UNIQUE SERIES
# FOR EVERY WOMAN YOU ARE...

## *Silhouette Romance*®

Tender, delightful, provocative—stories that capture the laughter, the tears, the *joy* of falling in love. Pure romance...straight from the heart!

## SILHOUETTE *Desire*®

Go wild with Desire! Passionate, emotional, sensuous stories of fiery romance. With heroines you'll like and heroes you'll *love,* Silhouette Desire never fails to deliver.

## *Silhouette Special Edition*®

Stories of love and life, these powerful novels are tales that you can identify with—romances with "something special" added in! Silhouette Special Edition is entertainment for the heart.

## SILHOUETTE·INTIMATE·MOMENTS®

Enter a world where passions run hot and excitement is the rule. Dramatic, larger-than-life and always compelling—Silhouette Intimate Moments will never let you down.                                                    SGENERIC